MIDLOTHIAN LIBRARIES

901343661   9

HB

MIDLOTHIAN LIBRARY SERV

Please return/renew this item~~~~ To
renew please give y~~~~ ay
be made in person, ~~~~.
www.mi~~~~

D0809839

STA 11/16
PSH 5/17
CC 7/17
BDC 10/17
SV 1/18
MOBILE

MIDLOTHIAN COUNCIL LIBRARY
WITHDRAWN

SPECIAL MESSAGE TO READERS

THE ULVERSCROFT FOUNDATION
(registered UK charity number 264873)

was established in 1972 to provide funds for research, diagnosis and treatment of eye diseases.
Examples of major projects funded by the Ulverscroft Foundation are:-

- The Children's Eye Unit at Moorfields Eye Hospital, London
- The Ulverscroft Children's Eye Unit at Great Ormond Street Hospital for Sick Children
- Funding research into eye diseases and treatment at the Department of Ophthalmology, University of Leicester
- The Ulverscroft Vision Research Group, Institute of Child Health
- Twin operating theatres at the Western Ophthalmic Hospital, London
- The Chair of Ophthalmology at the Royal Australian College of Ophthalmologists

You can help further the work of the Foundation by making a donation or leaving a legacy.
Every contribution is gratefully received. If you would like to help support the Foundation or require further information, please contact:

THE ULVERSCROFT FOUNDATION
The Green, Bradgate Road, Anstey
Leicester LE7 7FU, England
Tel: (0116) 236 4325
website: www.foundation.ulverscroft.com

MURDER DOWN EAST

Rich spinster Abbie Starr dies in her mansion without leaving a will. Her fortune is thought to have been converted into securities that have been hidden in the mansion — but searches there fail to find anything except a big overdraft. The courts give what is left to cousins Jenny Starr and Elsie Garry, allowing them to run the mansion as a boarding house. But when Jenny is found murdered, the evidence points to Elsie as the killer . . .

*Books by Victor Rousseau
in the Linford Mystery Library:*

THE WHITE LILY MURDER
THE MAN WITH THE CAMERA EYES

VICTOR ROUSSEAU

MURDER DOWN EAST

Complete and Unabridged

9 013436619

LINFORD
Leicester

First published in Great Britain

First Linford Edition
published 2016

Copyright © 1922, 1934 by Victor Rousseau
Copyright © 2016 by the Estate of
Victor Rousseau
All rights reserved

A catalogue record for this book is available
from the British Library.

ISBN 978–1–4448–2989–1

Published by
F. A. Thorpe (Publishing)
Anstey, Leicestershire

Set by Words & Graphics Ltd.
Anstey, Leicestershire
Printed and bound in Great Britain by
T. J. International Ltd., Padstow, Cornwall

This book is printed on acid-free paper

Contents

Murder Down East....................1

Woman and the Law 127

Murder Down East

1

The Lost Legacy

Martinfield, Maine, was quite a town once, when its clippers sailed the Seven Seas. It stands at the foot of high bluffs, intersected by the Plough River. Along the harbor front Main Street runs, with short cross-streets running back to the heights, and at their most precipitous point a long flight of wooden stairs leads up to the summit.

Here a few modern houses have been built, but many of them are at least a century old, and some are very large, and falling into decrepitude. Typical among these is the Starr mansion, built by Joshua Starr about the time when one William Pitt was championing the cause of the Colonies in the British Parliament, and the events of Bunker Hill and Lexington might already have been dimly descried in the distance.

Joshua Starr was a Loyalist; so, when farmers and redcoats began to mix things up in New England, the country people cut off the tails of his cows, and showed their displeasure in other ways. It was always suspected that he was implicated in the escape of a score of British prisoners from the old fort below the bluffs; in the end, he left the country and settled in Canada, where all his cows remained in possession of everything that nature had given them.

He turned his coat after Saratoga, and somehow managed to reinstate himself in the good will of the Government, so that, at the end of the war, he was once more in occupancy of the mansion on the heights. Suspect he remained until the end of his life, but his son, the clipper builder, became established as one of Martinfield's most respected citizens. The family fortune grew and grew, while the heirs dwindled.

By the year 1865 the big mansion and some three million dollars had passed into the sole ownership of Abigail Starr, an infant of eight months, an orphan, and the last of the direct line.

Toward the end of the first quarter of the twentieth century, Main Street looked very much as it had done fifty years before, except for the new banks and insurance offices near the Plough River bridge, while the Starr mansion, considerably weather-worn, still stood in its sagging picket fence, surrounded by a belt of gloomy trees, on the top of the bluff. A few houses had sprung up in its vicinity; there was Mr. Spumetti's tonsorial parlor, a grocery further back, a tethered goat or two, a quantity of litter — otherwise no change.

The steps that led down from the unpaved street at whose end the mansion stood descended into State Street near Main. Here, an old building housed two general medical practitioners; three ear, eye, nose and throat specialists; Lambert Van Houten and three other lawyers; a couple of realtors; and four insurance men.

Opposite was the shop of Frank Hubbard, mortician, with a small mortuary chapel adjoining, and at the rear of the premises was the morgue, which was nothing less than the ancient fort of Revolutionary days, a circular stone structure with loopholes and small barred windows, with a guardhouse which Mr. Hubbard used as a laboratory.

Frank Hubbard, a man of about fifty years, impeccably dressed in a suit of dark material, with a faint pin stripe in it, was looking out of the window in front of his office, facing on State Street.

As a thin, elderly, gray-haired woman passed along the street, carrying a large mesh bag, in which were a number of packages, he spoke to his assistant, Crome, an elderly man in a shabby suit, whom he had employed for about a year.

'There goes Miss Jenny Starr,' he said, 'carrying home her parcels. I guess she's having a hard time making both ends meet.'

Crome rubbed his lank cheek. 'I dunno. She's got Mr. Van Houten and Mr. Forrest, and that Mrs. Bennett who came yesterday. And Elsie Garry — I bet Jenny Starr pays her hardly anything — works for her like a slave.'

6

'What sort of woman is this Mrs. Bennett?' asked Hubbard. 'She seems a nice, quiet sort of person. Trained nurse, she says, and just finished a case in the country, an old gentleman she was with for a year. I heard Miss Jenny ask for her week's money in advance. I reckon Miss Jenny manages to make both ends meet, after a fashion.'

'If Jenny Starr and Elsie Garry had any sense,' said Hubbard, 'they'd sell the place. It ought to bring in enough over and above the bank's mortgage for them to start a boarding house in a better section of the town. It's a wonder to me Miss Jenny gets any boarders at all, in that ramshackle old place up on the bluff.'

'It's cheap,' said Crome. 'And handy for me.' He cackled. 'Reckon Miss Jenny ain't given up all hope of finding Miss Abbie Starr's money and securities,' he said. 'That kind of woman don't give up while life lasts. She's been at it nearly two years now, and she must have spent a mint of money pulling down the insides of the house, looking for the hiding place.'

'Two years?' said Hubbard, meditatively.

'Can it be two years since Abbie Starr died? It seems only yesterday the baker's man found her lying dead in her kitchen. Poor soul, there wasn't a solitary mourner at her burial.'

'I've heard she and Mr. Van Houten were sweethearts once, in the long ago,' said Crome. 'He was her lawyer and executor, wasn't he? He ought to have looked out for her property better.'

'I've heard he could never get her to make a will,' said Hubbard. 'She was mighty secretive. Just the sort of woman who would have hidden her securities away, instead of putting them in a safety deposit box, though I don't believe there's anything in that rumor. Miss Jenny would have found them, if there was.'

'That crowd of distant relatives who came after Abbie Starr's money must have looked mighty sore when they learned there wasn't anything,' cackled old Crome.

Hubbard smiled tolerantly. 'Human nature, Crome, human nature,' he answered.

'Yes, there was quite a stir when it turned out there wasn't anything but the mansion, and a big overdraft. The bank took a mortgage to cover that, which left practically nothing.'

'And the courts gave what there was to Miss Jenny and Elsie Garry, as next of kin,' reminisced Crome. 'And Miss Jenny got the bank to let her run the mansion as a boarding house. And she pulls the whole place to pieces, looking for Abbie Starr's fortune. But can you tell me why a well-to-do gentleman like Mr. Van Houten should go there to board, if he ain't after anything?'

'I guess Mr. Van Houten likes old associations. The Van Houten house stood next to the Starr mansion years ago, before it was pulled down by that millionaire who went bankrupt before he could start the foundations of the new home he'd planned.'

'There's a curse on the whole place,' snorted Crome. 'Everybody's crazy about Abbie Starr's fortune. A pack of fools, I call them. If they did find anything, it would go to Miss Jenny.'

'And Elsie Garry,' added the mortician.

'Elsie Garry was raised in the mansion, wasn't she?'

'She was born there. The mother died

just a week before Abbie. Elsie must have been eighteen then. Naturally, she wanted the mansion sold, being joint heir with Miss Jenny, so as to get her share of what was coming, and take a business course.'

'Yep, and Miss Jenny persuaded Elsie to stay with her and help her run the place as a boarding house instead,' Crome cackled, 'and they fight like dog and cat. I don't see how Elsie Garry can stand for that woman. Look, there goes Mr. Van Houten!'

An elderly, stooped man, with a gray goatee, had emerged from the building across the way. He moved slowly, nervously, toward the steps running up to the bluff. In his old-fashioned morning coat and derby, nobody would have guessed that the lawyer was reputed to be one of the wealthiest men in Martinfield. The two watched him go by.

'And there's Bill Forrest from the bank,' said Hubbard, as a good-looking young fellow passed briskly along the opposite side of State Street.

Crome's cackle rang out again. 'He's sweet on Miss Elsie,' he said. 'That's reason enough why he stays up to the mansion. Miss Jenny don't like it, but she can't afford to lose him.'

'I guess she can't stop Elsie Garry from marrying, if she wants to,' said the mortician. 'Forrest will get a good girl, and he'll be lucky. And now that we've seen Miss Jenny's boarders home, I guess we'll close up,' he added, sardonically.

He passed through his funeral parlor into the mortuary, switching on the light as he did so. The cluster of bulbs in the roof only seemed to accentuate the dreariness of the place, with its barred windows and the ancient loopholes, through which many a musket had been fired in the Revolutionary War. In three or four places around the walls the heavy iron staples, to which the prisoners' fetters had been attached, still remained firmly embedded in the stone.

Two raised stone slabs, jutting out into the center of the circular fort, stood ready for the reception of the dead. But Frank Hubbard did not seem to feel the dismal atmosphere of the place. He looked about him with an air of melancholy satisfaction.

2

Love — and Death

Miss Jenny Starr set a fairly good table, considering her few boarders. She could easily have accommodated fifteen persons in the rambling old mansion, and she had never had more than a half dozen at one time. At present she had four — Van Houten, the lawyer, who had lived there since the mansion had been reopened, eighteen months previously; Bill Forrest; Mrs. Bennett, the newcomer; and old Crome. In addition, there was the girl, Elsie Garry.

The dining room was huge. It looked out, on one side, over the bluff, and, in front, over an unpaved street. The windows were shrouded with heavy red curtains, which must have been there for at least a score of years. The electric light was dim, for Miss Jenny Starr, who had had electricity installed, found it necessary to keep her bills down as low as possible. The floor was new. Miss Jenny had had the old floor ripped up in her search for Abbie Starr's missing fortune.

The paper on the walls, had it been removed, would have shown pine planks inserted here and there into the old oak. Miss Jenny's search, though futile, had been thorough. Every room in the mansion had been investigated in the same way, especially the one Miss Jenny occupied, next to Elsie Garry's, on the ground floor behind the kitchen, for in this one Abbie Starr had lived for something like twenty years of solitary seclusion.

To Bill Forrest, the particular — in fact, the only — bright feature in the gloomy old house was Elsie Garry. Elsie was about twenty years of age, and, in Bill's eyes, she was an angel. Elsie was the only reason why Bill lived in the Starr mansion. He had gone there in the first place to save money, for Miss Jenny's rates were the lowest in town, and he liked a spacious room. But Miss Jenny's shrewish temper would have been too much for Bill, if Elsie hadn't been there.

He disliked old Crome and Van Houten, and they disliked him and each other, with the usual boarding house bitterness. Bill looked with annoyance at old Van Houten, occupying the head of the table, silent as usual, and apparently oblivious of the fact that there was another person in the room; at old Crome, gobbling his food, with napkin tucked under his chin; and at the demure Mrs. Bennett, eating in silence opposite him.

'Well, Forrest, how's the graphology coming along?' asked Crome, with a sneering cackle.

'The graphology,' Bill answered, 'is coming along quite nicely, thank you.'

'Did you get that weekly column in the Portsmouth *Echo* you were expecting?'

'I did,' said Bill. 'I am to have one every Saturday.' And, as he spoke, he saw Elsie, in the kitchen doorway, her face alight with pride and happiness. That weekly column meant ten dollars a week more on Bill's income, and the understanding between Bill and Elsie was sufficiently definite for her to understand the column's significance for them both.

'I don't altogether believe in palmistry,' tittered Mrs. Bennett. 'I may be wrong, of course, but I don't see how you can tell a person's destiny from his hand.'

'Graphology is not palmistry,' explained Bill, patiently. 'It is the science of hand-writing, and it has many practical applications, particularly that of enabling one to identify forged signatures and anonymous letters.'

'It looks as if this town has a good detective wasted in the First National,' cackled Crome.

'It has,' returned Bill, with composure. 'But the bank business happens to pay better. Thank you, Elsie, no more coffee.' And, since no formalities were wasted at the boarding house, Bill left the room.

It was three-quarters of an hour later when a slight figure stole out of the house to meet Bill Forrest, who was seated on one of the rustic seats that encircled the two old maples in the grassless yard.

'Oh, Bill, it made me so happy to hear you say that you've got that column!' said Elsie. 'That will mean a lot, won't it?'

'You bet it will,' said Bill, slipping his

15

arm around her as she sat down.
'Especially in the early fall — say about
September.' He kissed her.

'Bill, you don't know how glad I'll be to
leave this place,' said Elsie. 'I just can't
stand Cousin Jenny any longer. She does
nothing but scold. She's been crazy since
— you won't whisper a word about it,
Bill, will you?'

'Not even a syllable,' said Bill.

'She found one of Cousin Abbie's rings
last week, and all her hopes have been
revived.'

'Where did she find it?'

'You'll never guess. It had slipped
behind the board of the bottom drawer of
the old bureau in her room. It must have
been lying there all this time. It's a
beautiful diamond and an emerald. Such
stones! It must be worth a thousand
dollars. I can remember that Abbie Starr
always used to wear it. I believe it was the
ring Mr. Van Houten gave her years ago,
when they were engaged.

'And now Cousin Jenny's talking about
pulling the whole house to pieces to look
for that missing fortune. Oh, I don't see

how I can stand her even till September, Bill!'

'Why don't you force her to sell, and get your share of the property?' asked Bill.

'I don't like to. Poor woman, she's just hipped on the subject of that fortune. Of course there *isn't* any fortune. And, anyway, the place wouldn't bring in more than the amount of the mortgage.'

'I'm not so sure,' said Bill. 'The way property is beginning to pick up, I shouldn't be surprised if there mightn't be three or four thousand over to divide between you. I suppose you know,' he added, 'that your cousin couldn't meet the last interest on the mortgage?'

'No, I didn't know. Cousin Jenny never tells me a thing. But I know she's been terribly worked up today about something. There was an odd-looking letter came for her this morning, written in pencil, and forwarded from Hobart, where she used to live. Mrs. Bennett took in the mail, and Cousin Jenny snatched it out of her hands and acted like a crazy woman when she saw that letter. She's been wild all day.

'I don't care, I'll be glad to be out of here. Cousin Jenny hasn't paid me a penny for months, and I don't know how I'm going to get any clothes this fall,' Elsie sighed.

'You should worry about clothes or anything else, with that column of mine starting next month,' grinned Bill. 'Ten solid iron men every week, and with my salary, that makes forty-five, Elsie.'

'Oh, Bill, that's wonderful! But somehow I just can't bring myself to force Cousin Jenny to lose the house.'

'Maybe she'll have to, if she can't catch up on that interest,' Bill said. 'Anyhow, you see she doesn't gyp you out of what's coming to you. Now kiss me again.'

Elsie complied, then drew back quickly, as a shadow detached itself from the house door and moved along the path toward the gate. It was Mr. Van Houten, neat and old-fashioned as ever, in his cutaway and derby. He passed Bill and Elsie, apparently without seeing them, and sauntered toward the steps. He often went down to his office in the evening, though his clients consisted mainly of a mere handful of old-fashioned citizens of Martinfield.

'Elsie,' said Bill, 'will September suit you? Soon after Labor Day?'

'Oh, Bill!' said Elsie.

An emphatic cough behind them made them both jump. The figure of Jenny Starr appeared; evidently she had been standing on the other side of the big maple tree for quite a little time.

'So I'm a *pest*, am I, Mr. Forrest?' she said shrilly. 'Well, some of us have the same opinion about *other* folks. You can leave here tomorrow morning, and go somewhere where things are more to your liking. I've had my eyes on you for some time past.'

'I hope your visions were not unpleasant, Miss Starr,' said Bill, politely.

'Don't you *dare* to talk back to me!' shrilled Miss Jenny. 'I know your kind, making love to my cousin because you think she's going to be a rich woman some day! And she a beggar whom I took in out of charity!'

Bill's face grew red. 'Say, Miss Starr, I guess you're letting your tongue run away with your judgment,' he answered. 'Elsie's just as much a beggar as you are.'

'And that's true! Half this property is *mine*. And half that ring you found is mine, if it comes to that!' Elsie cried, forgetting herself in her anger.

'You leaving me to put the dishes away, so that you could steal out and let *him* make love to you!' shouted Miss Jenny angrily, going off on a new tack. 'You'll come right back and finish your work, d'you hear me?'

'I'll come back,' retorted Elsie. 'But I tell you right now I'm through with you. I'm not a hired girl, and you've no right to treat me the way you do!'

Without another word, Elsie started back for the house, Jenny Starr following her and muttering to herself furiously. Halfway to the door, she turned and shot over her shoulder:

'You can leave in the morning, Mr. Forrest, and good riddance to you!'

Bill, without replying, went inside and up to his room, which was over Elsie's. His blood was boiling, but after a while he cooled down, put on his dressing gown, and began to reflect quite practically over the situation.

He had several hundred dollars in the bank, and he was good for forty-five a week. In the morning he'd ask Elsie to come away with him and get married. By nightfall next day they could be established in a snug little furnished apartment, one of the new ones that were going up on Littlefield Street. His pulses leaped at the prospect.

'I wonder what was in that letter,' he mused.

He spent some time going over a book of graphology, and then went to bed. But for a long time he was kept awake by the sound of the two women's voices from below. Jenny Starr was keeping up an incessant monologue, which appeared to come, now from her own room, and now from Elsie's. Now and again Bill could hear Elsie's indignant replies. But after a while he fell asleep.

Then suddenly he was sitting up in his bed. Had that been a dream, or had a single, shrill shriek of agony rung through the house?

He leaped out of bed, thrust his feet into his slippers, and wrapped his dressing gown about him. He knew that shriek had been no dream. For other cries were coming from the ground floor, Elsie's cries for help, cries of wild terror.

Footsteps sounded along the hall. Old Crome appeared in a pair of faded pajamas, and behind him the form of Mrs. Bennett.

'What was that?' cried the nurse. 'Oh, God, listen to her!'

'G-g-go down, Forrest,' chattered old Crome. 'Somebody's being murdered!'

Bill rushed down the stairs, through the dining, room and kitchen, into Jenny Starr's room. Thank God, Elsie was unharmed! She was standing beside the bed, wringing her hands and crying helplessly.

The room was lit only by the moonlight that filtered in through the maples. It showed the bed, and, on it, the contorted figure of Jenny Starr, from which something was dripping, dripping to the floor.

'Turn on the light, quick, for God's sake!' shouted Van Houten behind Bill.

Bill found the switch and clicked it.

The glare of the electric light drowned the moonlight. Bill could see Jenny Starr lying motionless in the midst of a crimson stain, with one blade of a pair of shears buried to the hilt in her heart, through her night dress.

3

The Ring

It seemed an eternity, though it could not have been more than twenty minutes, before the police car chugged up to the door, and two officers leaped out. One was Detective Ralston, a youngish man, a few years older than Bill, with whom he was on terms of friendly acquaintance. The other was Police Chief Emery, who had had charge in Martinfield for half a generation; white-haired, with a clipped white mustache; a man quite efficient in a practical, unimaginative way.

During that eternity, Bill had been holding Elsie, who was sobbing incoherently. Van Houten and old Crome were hysterical. Mrs. Bennett had collapsed in a faint, and was lying upon the lounge in the dining room.

The ticking clock upon the mantel in the bedroom marked four o'clock.

24

Almost coincidently with the police car arrived Doctor Johnson, for whom Van Houten had telephoned. Johnson held the office of coroner, and lived on Quigley Street, round the corner from his office on State, just at the bottom of the steps. He was a bachelor, and well liked in Martinfield.

Chief of Police Emery cast a glance at the quiet figure on the bed, but no exclamation escaped his tight-shut lips. 'Anything been touched?' he asked.

'Not a thing,' answered Bill.

'How'd it happen?'

Bill told of the scream that had awakened him, and old Crome, who was still badly shaken, corroborated his story. Also Van Houten, whose room adjoined Elsie's, though there was no door between. He had hurried in through the dining room and kitchen, in the wake of Bill, to find Elsie standing by the dead woman in the moonlight.

'This your room, Miss Garry?' asked Emery, indicating the small room at the back. 'Let's hear your story, then.' As he spoke, he moved to the single window of

Jenny Starr's room. The window was up, but the screen was nailed in position, and had evidently not been tampered with. Detective Ralston was in the kitchen adjoining.

'It's just as these people have told,' said Elsie, shuddering. 'I was awakened by hearing Cousin Jenny scream. I sprang out of bed and tried to open the door between our rooms, but you see it's locked.'

Emery moved to the door and tried the lock. The key was in it on the side of Jenny Starr's bedroom, and he had to turn it to get the door open. The electric light shone into Elsie's room, showing the small, rumpled bed.

'How did you get in here?' asked Emery.

'I ran out to the porch behind my room, and pushed up one of the kitchen windows. I saw Cousin Jenny lying there, and — and I don't remember anything more except screaming, until the rest came.'

'Did your cousin usually lock the door between your rooms?' asked Emery.

26

'Never — never before, that I can remember. But she was mad at me last night, and upset about things.'

Emery looked at the girl with a frowning stare. Then for the first time Bill realized that there was blood on her hands and negligée, and on his own hands, too.

'You touched her?'

'I must have done so. I — I don't know what I did. I lost my head. It's so terrible!' Elsie wept.

'Think, now! Did you try to pull out the scissors?'

'I don't know. No, of course not. I don't know that I even saw what it was that had killed her.'

Meanwhile, Johnson had been wiping away the blood about the wound. He turned around. He was a shortish man of about forty, with a clipped brown beard and a bald forehead, and a pair of deep-set gray eyes.

'Killed instantly, or practically instantly,' he said. 'Right through the heart. You see, there's blood all over the handles of these shears. No chance of fingerprints here.

27

The blow must have been struck with terrific force.'

Ralston came in from the next room.

'One window up in the kitchen, none in the dining room,' he said. 'Looks like the killer came in that way. But there's no signs of footprints, Chief, and it's been raining heavily.'

He glanced down at his own mud-stained boots, then at Emery's. He shrugged his shoulders.

'The porch is dry and wouldn't show foot-tracks,' he said. 'But if the person who did this job came from outside, then he must have put on rubbers when he came in.'

'I can tell you something!' Mrs. Bennett came tottering into the room, and stood leaning against the door jamb. Her voice was hysterical. 'I don't think you'll have to look very far for the person who killed Jenny Starr,' she cried. 'My room's right above this one, and every sound comes up that chimney.'

She pointed to the large brick chimney in the room, set into an angle between the door of Elsie's room and the window. In its deep recess a dozen logs could have been laid, but it had not been used for years, and Jenny Starr had kept the massive grate and heavy andirons blacked and polished.

'I heard her and Elsie Garry quarreling for hours after I went to bed. I couldn't sleep because of the racket,' the nurse went on. 'It started right after dinner, when she caught Elsie Garry and this man kissing out in the yard. Miss Jenny Starr told him he could leave in the morning. Then they started quarreling all over again over that ring that Jenny Starr had found — '

'What ring?' snapped Emery.

'Why, it was one of Abbie Starr's rings. Miss Jenny had found it somewhere. I heard Elsie Garry claiming that she had a half-right to it. They were fighting about it like a couple of cats.'

'It's not true!' cried Elsie. 'I — she — '

Chief Emery silenced her. 'Go on, please,' he said to Mrs. Bennett.

'Then Elsie Garry demanded that the house should be sold, so that she could have her half of the money, and poor

Jenny Starr pleaded with her not to insist.'

'What about this ring?' Emery asked Elsie.

'It's a ring my cousin found in the back of a drawer,' answered the girl. 'It must have been there since Cousin Abbie died. But we didn't quarrel about it. I only said that half of the value belonged to me. And it's not true that we were quarreling, as she says. Cousin Jenny was overwrought, and she came into my room after we'd gone to bed, and began scolding me.'

'Mind if we look through your room, Miss Garry?' Emery nodded to Ralston, without waiting for the girl's answer, and the detective went quickly through and closed the door behind him. The electric light from Elsie's room shone underneath it.

'Now who else heard this quarrel?' asked Emery, looking at Bill.

'I heard some sort of argument,' Bill admitted. 'My room is above Miss Garry's. But it wasn't anything I'd never heard before.'

'How about yourself, Mr. Van Houten?'

30

asked the Police Chief. 'Where's your room?'

'On the ground floor, on the other side of the house,' answered the lawyer. 'It adjoins this one and Miss Elsie's. Yes, I heard what sounded like an altercation, I must admit.'

Emery nodded and turned back. 'What were those shears used for?' he asked Elsie.

'They're just a pair of old shears that Cousin Jenny kept in the kitchen. They're all blunted, and she used them for cutting strings and sometimes opening cans.'

'When did you see them last?'

'I don't know. Yesterday, I suppose. I don't remember. How can I remember?'

'Now take it easy, Miss Garry,' said Emery. 'We're only trying to get some light on this business. Whoever killed Miss Jenny Starr must have come in through the kitchen . . . Now what about the ring?'

'It was she who brought up that subject. She said that she was sure we'd got on the trail of Cousin Abbie's fortune, and I'd be a fool to force her to let the house get into the hands of strangers. And she said she'd found the ring, and findings were keepings. At last she stamped out of my room and locked the door behind her.'

'Where is this ring?'

'She hid it somewhere. I've seen it only once.'

'Mr. Emery!' came Detective Ralston's voice from Elsie's room. He flung the door open. 'Will you step in here, please?'

There was something ominous and grim in the detective's voice that made everyone surge forward in the wake of the police chief. The electric bulb was over Elsie's bureau, and Ralston was holding something in his right hand, with his left hand behind him. It was a compact.

'Found it in here, tucked away in the bottom drawer, under a pile of clothes,' said Ralston, opening the compact, which was empty, save for a small circular patch of rouge. 'And this was in it!'

Ralston brought forward his left hand and opened it. In it was the ring, with a large diamond and an emerald in an old-fashioned setting. The value of the ring must have been two thousand dollars.

A strangled cry broke from Van Houten's throat. 'I — I gave Abbie Starr that!' he exclaimed hoarsely. 'Forty years ago it must have been. She always wore it when I came to see her — after we became reconciled a few years ago.'

But the eyes of all were turned upon Elsie. For a moment, the girl stood staring at the ring as if paralyzed.

'I lost that compact last week,' she cried. 'I never put that ring in it. I — I — oh, Bill, tell me that you believe I'm speaking the truth!'

Bill put his arm around her. 'You bet I do, and so does everybody else here,' he said, defiantly. 'Maybe your cousin slipped that ring in there to surprise you,' he ventured.

Mrs. Bennett's tittering laugh broke the silence. Nobody spoke. Chief Emery cleared his throat.

'I'm mighty sorry, Miss Garry,' he said. 'I guess all this will be cleared up, but I'll have to ask you to get dressed quick.'

'You mean you're placing her under

arrest for murdering her cousin?' Bill demanded. 'Damn it, have a little sense! Why, look at her! Just look at her!'

'Just get dressed quick, Miss Garry,' was all that Emery answered. He nodded to Ralston, who went through the door at the opposite end of the bedroom, leading to the porch, to take up his guard outside. 'Come along, leave Miss Garry alone,' he said, and the rest trooped out, Bill, after a despairing glance at Elsie, following them.

The door was closed. Bill looked at Emery, at Van Houten, Crome, Mrs. Bennett. He was dazed. Suddenly it dawned upon him that every other person in that room had believed from the beginning that Elsie had murdered Jenny Starr.

Emery came up to Bill. 'Now take it easy, Forrest,' he said.

He said something more, but Bill didn't know what it was. He couldn't pull himself together. He was still looking about him in bewilderment, when the door opened again, and Elsie appeared, dressed, and carrying a little bag in her hand.

'I'm ready,' she said to Emery, then ran

to Bill. 'Oh, Bill, so long as you know it isn't true, I don't care — I don't care!' she sobbed.

Bill held her tight. 'True?' he cried. 'Of course it isn't true! But I'll tell you what is true. I'm going to run down the murderous hound who did this thing, if it takes me a year.'

The silence that followed was broken by Mrs. Bennett's nervous titter. It sounded malicious.

4

Public Opinion

A jury of twelve of Martinfield's citizens, presided over by Doctor Johnson, had brought in a verdict that Jenny Starr had come to her death at the hands of Elsie Garry.

Elsie hadn't been at the inquest. She had suffered a nervous collapse in her cell, and had been given a strong sleeping sedative. Late in the afternoon Bill went to the police station, where he was at once admitted to Emery's private room.

He found him with Sims, the prosecuting attorney. Sims was a jumpy little man, with a square face and bulldog jaw, a newcomer in Martinfield, and anxious to make a reputation. They both seemed glad to see Bill, and they let him talk.

Bill had been asserting Elsie's innocence for about five minutes before he realized that Sims was craftily leading him on to commit himself to some damaging statement about the girl.

'I'm going to talk to you frankly, Forrest,' said Sims, when Bill's flow of speech had stopped. 'Your evidence at the inquest was not entirely satisfactory. You gave the impression that you could have shed further light on the motive for the murder, if you had been willing to do so.'

'I tell you again, Miss Garry's innocent,' said Bill. 'She's simply incapable of committing a dastardly crime like that. And for what motive? A ring!'

'How long have you been engaged to her?' inquired Sims, blandly.

'I don't know. Three or four weeks perhaps.'

'Miss Garry must have talked to you about her position at the mansion. Is it credible, I ask you, that she said nothing to you about Miss Starr's having found that ring?'

'She did speak to me about it. She told me about it only last night. Why shouldn't she have told me about it?' Bill demanded.

'Didn't she speak enviously about it,

and say she thought she had as much right to it as Jenny Starr, or, at any rate, that it should be sold, and the value divided equally?' the attorney persisted.

'Certainly not,' said Bill. 'But if she had said anything of the sort, she would have been perfectly justified in doing so.'

'She didn't express her hatred for her cousin and wish that she was out of the way?'

'I tell you, she never said anything of the kind!' Bill stormed. 'You can't put testimony like that into my mouth. All she said was that she was unhappy with Miss Starr, and then I asked her to marry me soon. I told her, too, that she should insist on Miss Starr's selling and dividing the receipts equally. Jenny Starr hadn't paid her a penny for months.'

The look of satisfaction on Sims' face checked him. He was shocked into wariness. He realized now that it was impossible to hope for sympathy from anyone. They were all firmly convinced that Elsie had killed her cousin. He would have to play a lone hand.

He turned to Emery. 'Surely you don't

believe she's guilty?' he asked.

'Now see here, my boy,' replied the police chief, 'I can only go upon evidence. The murder was an inside job. Even if the murderer had come from outside and worn rubbers, they'd have left tracks in that mud. Somebody in the house killed Jenny Starr. Who had any motive except Miss Garry? You? Mr. Van Houten? Crome? Mrs. Bennett?'

Looking up, Bill saw an extraordinary expression on Sims' face at that moment. He knew that the man was bent upon a verdict of murder in the first degree, and that he would send Elsie to her death with as little compunction as he would drown a kitten. Sims leaned forward and shook his finger in Bill's face.

'I'll tell you frankly, Forrest, I've been considering holding you as a material witness,' he said. 'Don't try to leave Martinfield until the trial is over.'

'I'm not leaving Martinfield,' Bill retorted. 'And let me tell you, Miss Garry's going to be acquitted.'

'Yes? And what brings you to that conclusion?' inquired the prosecuting attorney, blandly.

'The evidence against her is just a little too perfect,' answered Bill, 'especially the planting of that ring in her bureau.'

He got up, moved slowly toward the door, while the two men watched him. Then he stopped, turned back.

'I suppose I can have a permit to see Miss Garry?' he asked Emery.

Emery looked at Sims, who shook his head decisively.

'Not today, Forrest,' he answered. 'In fact, Miss Garry is in no condition to see anybody. I'll see what can be done for you tomorrow.'

'But she's got to have a lawyer!' Bill shouted.

Neither of the two answered him, and Bill stamped through into the station.

Detective Ralston was sitting on a bench. The desk was empty, nobody else was in the room. Ralston was a keen-minded young fellow, and Bill had occasionally discussed his hobby of graphology with him. He got up and beckoned to Bill, glancing toward the inner door. Almost at once, however, the door was pushed to.

'I'm sorry, Forrest,' said Ralston. 'I heard what Sims just said to you. As a matter of fact, the doctor gave Miss Garry a pretty strong opiate, and the matron was saying just now that she hasn't come out of it yet. I guess Sims will give you permission to see her tomorrow. If he won't, you can apply to a judge, you know.

'I just hate to be in on this business, Forrest. Everybody knows Miss Garry, and a nicer girl never breathed. If she's innocent, the truth will come out. Who's she got for a lawyer?'

'I haven't been to see one yet,' said Bill. 'Whom would you recommend?'

'I tell you, you can't beat Hickson,' said Ralston. 'He's pretty keen. He's got off more fellows than any other lawyer in town. I'd try to see him before his office closes. It's in the new Commerce Building.'

'Thanks,' said Bill. 'I'm sure much obliged to you, Ralston. Only get it into your head that Miss Garry's innocent.' He strode out of the station. Ralston looked after him and shook his head. He couldn't believe in Elsie's innocence. Who could, when she was simply snowed under by the weight of evidence?

Bill had heard of Hickson as a man with a flair for ferreting out the weak points of a prosecution; in fact, he had had him in mind, even before Ralston spoke of him. He made his way along Main Street, fully aware that he was being recognized by scores among the crowds, and that heads were craned to follow his progress. He took the elevator up to the third floor of the Commerce Building.

'Mr. Hickson's engaged,' said the stenographer, who apparently failed to recognize him. 'I don't believe that he'll be free this afternoon.'

'Tell him I'll wait,' said Bill.

'What name, please?'

'Tell him Mr. William Forrest would like to see him about Miss Garry,' Bill replied.

The stenographer's eyes almost popped out of her head, and she sprang to her feet and hurried into the lawyer's private office.

'Mr. Hickson will be able to see you in

a few minutes,' she announced, when she returned, and began tapping the typewriter keys nervously, while Bill sat waiting.

It was no more than ten minutes before the door opened, and a rough-looking, red-faced man came out. In the doorway stood Hickson.

'Mr. Forrest?' he said. 'Please come inside.'

Hickson was a youngish man, clean-shaven, with a keen, alert look in his gray eyes. He shook hands with Bill cordially.

'You want to see me about this case?' he asked. 'On behalf of Miss Garry?'

'I want to ask you to represent her,' answered Bill. 'She doesn't know yet. In fact, she's still under the influence of an opiate they gave her. They wouldn't let me see her. She's innocent. And Sims is trying to secure a first-degree murder verdict.'

'Maybe it won't be so bad as you think,' suggested Hickson. 'Go ahead. Tell me everything in your own way.'

He listened while Bill talked, drumming his fingers on the polished mahogany top of his desk. Occasionally he intervened with a question, always pertinent and to the point.

'Of course, until I've talked with Miss Garry, I can't outline any course of defense,' he said at length. 'But it's notorious in town how Jenny Starr treated the girl. I believe we ought to be able to build up considerable sympathy for Miss Garry along that line. If we can show that the act was wholly unpremeditated, possibly committed in self-defense, there is the certainty of a manslaughter verdict, at the worst. There is even the possibility of an acquittal.'

Bill thumped his fist upon the table.

'Damn it, she's innocent!' he shouted. 'And there's no need for any tricks or subterfuges. She's innocent, and I want the guilty person tracked down.'

'A pretty big order,' answered the lawyer, 'with the whole force of the law bent on convicting Miss Garry.'

'I want you to do your best for me, anyway,' said Bill. 'Will you?'

Hickson drummed his fingers again and was silent for a while, Bill watching him with suspense. 'I'll take the case,' he announced. 'Yes, I'll take it. On one condition, though.'

'Go ahead and name it,' said Bill. 'I can put up five hundred cash — '

'I'm not thinking about the money just now. I'm willing to take the case on one condition. That is, that you step right out of the picture and leave me to make my own plans for the defense, after I've seen Miss Garry.'

'I won't stand for any plea of manslaughter,' said Bill, 'and you'll find Miss Garry won't either. She's innocent, and you'll believe it as soon as you've seen her.'

'I don't say that I intend to plead manslaughter. It is possible that Miss Garry may be innocent. I only know what I've read in the papers,' Hickson returned. 'I'm not going to commit myself until I've talked the whole matter over with her tomorrow. Then, if she and you decide to retain another lawyer, that will, of course, be your privilege.

'But in the meantime, you fade out of the picture, Forrest, and let me caution you *not* to say a single word to the press.

If Sims or Emery sends for you, refuse to be cross-examined, and *demand* to be put in touch with me.'

Bill thought pretty fast. He liked Hickson, and he believed he couldn't get a better man.

'I'll accept your terms, for the present,' he answered. 'Have your talk with Miss Garry tomorrow, and then we'll thresh it all out. But I'm telling you here and now, there will be no plea of manslaughter, because Miss Garry's innocent.'

Bill turned and strode out.

Leaving the lawyer's office, Bill found his clarity of mind returning. He realized now that he must rely in the main on himself. Everybody believed that Elsie was guilty of the murder. And even Bill had to admit that the evidence was damningly against her.

He realized that he had eaten nothing that day, and stopped at a lunch wagon at the foot of the bluff, and had a cup of coffee and a couple of sandwiches. He also bought the evening paper.

Nearly the whole of the front page was devoted to an account of the murder.

There were photographs of Elsie and Jenny Starr. Bill only glanced through the page. He hadn't the heart to read it. But one item stood out as clearly as if he had been directed to it.

Emily Bennett, the nurse, was reported to have left Martinfield secretly that afternoon, and it was hinted that a warrant might be issued for her apprehension as a material witness.

Bill read that with something of a shock. Was it possible that Mrs. Bennett had murdered Jenny Starr? Certainly her evidence against Elsie had been rancorous, and probably false. On the other hand, it was impossible that she could have slipped downstairs and killed the dead woman, and then run up the back stairs in time to appear at the door of his own bedroom as he emerged.

Mrs. Bennett and old Crome had been hard upon his heels when he went out into the passage. The dead woman's scream had hardly ceased to sound. No, it was incredible that Mrs. Bennett was the murderess.

Bill was surprised when he reached the

top of the bluffs to find that the crowd of morbid sightseers had disappeared, and that the house was apparently unguarded. He went into the house. No policeman or detective seemed to be on the premises.

The evidences of the murder had been removed, but the bloodstained sheets were still on Jenny Starr's bed, and her room had been ransacked thoroughly. Even the nailed-down carpet had been taken up and rolled to one side. Every scrap of correspondence had apparently been removed by the police, and there was nothing but the ransacked drawers and closet, and the heaps of tumbled clothing.

Bill went up to his own room. Immediately he discovered that it had been subjected to the same minute search. All his clothes lay in a tumbled heap upon his bed, and a number of letters had been pulled out of their envelopes and taken away. Even his graphology books were missing.

Bill didn't care. He sat down in the rocking chair and tried to focus his mind upon the problem. The more he thought, the more insoluble it appeared to be. He went downstairs again and examined the windows. The murderer could have come in only through the kitchen window — and he hadn't crossed the yard. The rain had churned up the earth into a swamp all around the house.

Bill could see only one possibility. Across the hall was the parlor, with Van Houten's room behind it. Was it possible that the ultra-respectable lawyer had had time to sneak in and commit the deed?

It was just possible. And Van Houten had handled Abbie Starr's affairs. If Jenny Starr had got on the track of any defalcations —

There were numerous possibilities, numerous angles, to be considered. But what a tangled maze to think through!

As Bill paced the dining room, thinking, a car came chugging along the road. It stopped in front of the house. Looking across the darkening yard, Bill recognized the roadster that Van Houten kept in an old stable at the rear of the house. Van Houten took the car out about three times a week, driving into town along the circuitous road that wound around the bluff and descended into the upper end of Main Street.

And Van Houten, in the morning coat and black derby, was stepping out of the roadster. Queer . . .

5

The Secret Entrance

Watching from behind the red curtains, Bill saw Van Houten enter the walk, then pass round to the side entrance of the house, which connected directly with his room at the back of the parlor.

The lawyer certainly looked a nervous wreck, so far as Bill was able to discern in the twilight. He moved erratically, he staggered from side to side as he walked. Bill waited till the man was in his room, then crossed the hall, went through the parlor, and tapped at Van Houten's door.

He heard a cry from within. 'Who's there?' called the lawyer, in a quavering voice.

'It's me, Bill Forrest.'

The door opened. Van Houten stood looking at him. The light over the desk had been switched on, and Bill could see that Van Houten was shaking like a palsied man. His face was the color of chalk. The room had not apparently been searched, but Van Houten had been collecting his things, and a couple of suitcases upon the bed were disgorging clothes and letters.

'What — what do you want?' Van Houten stammered. 'What have you come back here for? I — I came to get my things. I've had enough of this house for a lifetime.' He uttered a forced laugh. 'I guess you've been hit pretty badly, Forrest,' he said. 'I've got to have a drink. Maybe you'd like one, too.'

He took up a pint bottle of prescription whisky and poured a liberal quantity into a tumbler, with a hand that trembled violently. He picked up another glass, nearly dropping it in the process, and handed it and the bottle to Bill, who took a very small helping.

'I guess you know,' said Bill, when Van Houten had tossed off his drink, 'that Elsie Garry's innocent.'

Van Houten shook again. 'I can't believe it of her,' he muttered. 'She's not that kind of girl. I believe there's a hideous mistake somewhere.'

'Yeah,' said Bill, beginning to feel master of himself again. 'And it started with that letter that Jenny Starr received yesterday.'

The lawyer's look of innocent inquiry, if feigned, was perfect. 'What letter?'

'That's what I want to know,' said Bill. 'I know she got a letter written in pencil that upset her. Maybe she talked to you about it, since you were advising her. At least, she naturally would have.'

'Jenny Starr said nothing to me about any letter,' Van Houten protested.

'Maybe it had something to do with the fellow who's dickering for the house,' said Bill. 'I guess you know about him, anyway — name of Jones. Comes from Lowell, he says. Of course, he's a blind for someone else.'

'I tell you that Jenny Starr said nothing to me about any letter,' cried Van Houten.

'Of course,' Bill went on, 'having obtained that piece of information in the course of my duties at the bank, I wasn't in a position to make it public, even to inform Miss Garry.'

'Let's come to the point,' said Van Houten. 'What do you want?'

'I want Miss Garry freed from that murder charge,' answered Bill.

'What can I do?' cried the lawyer. 'Do you suppose that I know anything about the murder? Are you insinuating that I had any motive in wishing to see Jenny Starr killed? I don't know what you're driving at, young man, but let me tell you that there's such an offense as blackmail, and if you're trying to extort — '

Bill shrugged his shoulders. 'No need to take that line, Mr. Van Houten,' he answered. 'I'm out to free Miss Garry, and I thought you might be willing to cooperate. If you can't, or won't — '

'Forrest, I swear to you that if there was any way in which I could assist you, I'd do it, no matter what the cost to myself,' cried Van Houten vehemently. 'And maybe I can. I know a few tricks of the trade if you want me to undertake the girl's defense — '

'No,' said Bill, 'I've got Hickson. I'm out to get that letter. If you don't know about it, or won't tell, I'll just have to go on playing a lone hand.'

'I know nothing about any letter that Jenny Starr received!' the lawyer shouted.

'All right,' said Bill. 'I guess I was mistaken, then. We'll let it slide.'

Had Van Houten any knowledge of the contents of the missing letter? The man was in such a nervous state that it was impossible for Bill to draw any inference from his demeanor. Bill went back to his room. He saw Van Houten leave the house carrying his suitcases, and drive away. Bill was alone in the house now.

It had occurred to him that Jenny Starr might have burned the letter in the furnace, and he went downstairs through the door that led from the kitchen to the basement. It had grown quite dark, and the cellar was all but invisible.

Bill dared not switch on a light, but he struck a match and looked about him. The stone vault that was the cellar ran the whole length of the old house. At one end was the partition for storing coal, at the other were the shelves where food and provisions had been kept in the days before artificial ice came into existence.

Great hooks for hanging hams and game were still suspended from the ceiling. Through the little window on one side, hardly three feet above the rocks, one could look down upon the town below. Bill could see the lights of Martinfield strung out in a long array under him.

Toward one side of the cellar the big furnace had been set up at a time some twenty years before. Bill struck another match, opened the door, and peered inside it. The match was, however, almost instantly blown out by the strong draft that seemed to suck up the air from the interior. The furnace, with its flue, seemed to act as a sort of suction pump.

Bill struck a match again, guarding it carefully with his hand. The interior of the furnace still contained the ashes of the last spring fire, but on top of those ashes were little fragments of charred paper.

Someone, quite recently, had burned a letter or some paper inside — quite lately, for the ashes remained in a little heap on top of the burned-out coal. But even as Bill tried, very carefully, to raise them in his hands, the fragments rose and began circulating around the interior, finally whirling up the flue.

It was odd, that suction-pump effect, but Bill didn't know very much about furnaces. He knew, however, that, if those were the fragments of Jenny Starr's letter, there was now not the faintest chance of discovering what its contents had been.

In deep dejection he went up to his room again. He felt baffled and helpless. Again and again his mind ranged over all possible murderers — Van Houten, Mrs. Bennett, old Crome — only to reject each one.

A single street light stood on the opposite side of the unpaved road. Looking out through his window, Bill saw a solitary figure pass and repass it, looking up at the house. Bill grinned wryly. Nobody could mistake that figure for anyone but a detective, and a novice, at that. His presence in the house was known; he had been trailed; he was under surveillance.

And now Bill began to see why the house had not been placed under police guard. It was because he himself was under suspicion of being an accomplice in the murder of Jenny Starr! Sims hoped to fasten something upon him, and had laid the trap in the hope that he would step into it. The forces of malignant cunning that were arrayed against Elsie would stop at nothing.

Bill didn't care. He dropped upon his bed and lay there, staring with open eyes into the darkness. Hours passed, but he did not sleep, and hardly stirred.

It must have been in the middle of the night when Bill sat up suddenly, listening. He thought he had heard the sound of movements somewhere in the house. They seemed to come from Elsie's room, beneath his, or from the one that had been occupied by Jenny Starr.

A thud was audible. Somebody seemed to have stumbled over something. The sounds ceased. Bill crept to his door, moved to the head of the stairs that led up from the hall, and listened. He heard the unmistakable faint sounds of movements somewhere. There was someone in the house.

From his new position, it seemed that the sounds came from the right side of the hall, instead of the left — that is, from the parlor or Van Houten's room, instead of from the dining room, the kitchen, or the rooms that had been occupied by the two women. Van Houten back, perhaps searching for the letter! That was the immediate thought that leaped into Bill's mind.

Well, Van Houten was trapped this time, if it was Van Houten. Before he could make his getaway, Bill would have him. And this time he'd make the man talk!

Bill crept softly down the stairs, listening intently. He thought he had reached the hall. He put one foot down, and encountered nothing. There was a last step that he had overlooked. He stumbled and fell noisily upon the hall floor.

Instantly he heard the sound of soft, quick movements. And he had been dead wrong. The sounds had not come from Van Houten's room, but from the kitchen, or Jenny Starr's room. Footsteps went echoing softly through the house and died away. By the time Bill had regained his feet, he could hear nothing.

He leaped in pursuit, and almost hurled himself down the stairs that led to the basement. A dull metallic clang came to his ears. Then followed silence.

Bill crouched in the cellar, lit a match, and peered about him. The cellar looked empty, yet he was confident that the intruder had gone down into it.

He moved forward, striking matches as he did so, and risking the chance of a bullet. There was nobody in the place. Bill rushed the coal-bin, and found it empty. There was nowhere else where the intruder could be lurking.

The little window overlooking the rocks was too small for even a child to have squeezed through, and it was nailed fast, and had been nailed fast for years. On the opposite side of the cellar were two other windows, equally small. Bill investigated them, with the aid of matches. Both of these were nailed, too, and stuck fast, as well, with dirt that had solidified to the consistency of cement.

The intruder had not escaped that way. Besides, the clang seemed to have come from the furnace. Bill went to the furnace door.

At once he saw that a layer of fine ashes lay in front of it. And that layer had not been there before. There was only one inference to be drawn. Whoever had been in the cellar had either escaped through the furnace, or, at least, disturbed it.

But that was preposterous — unless the intruder was still hiding within. The door of the big furnace was just large enough for a man to squeeze into. Bill flung it open.

'Come out!' he shouted, not very convincingly, for a human body hidden within would certainly have bulged. And Bill's hand encountered only emptiness.

He struck another match and saw that the furnace was empty. He tried to look up, but the draft extinguished the flame instantly. Bill had seen, however, that the furnace connected simply with the hot-air pipes that radiated from it on all sides, and up to the roof of the cellar.

Bill drew back, sneezing, as the fine

dust settled in his nostrils. He was positive that the clang he had heard had come from the furnace. But it was impossible that anyone could be hiding in any of the lengths of stovepipe.

He struck another match. And then he made a singular discovery, so grotesque that it had simply not dawned on him before. At least, he *had* seen it, but it had made no impression upon him, because he had drawn no inference from it.

Nearly the entire heap of coal had disappeared from the furnace grate. There remained only little ridges heaped up at the sides, and the black bars of the grate extended from front to rear.

Bill leaned in, felt for the old-fashioned hinges of the grate, and lifted it. It dropped back into position with exactly the same clang that Bill had heard when the intruder made his getaway.

Bill stood back. His mind was clearing now. Somewhere beneath the grate of the furnace there was a secret passage leading to the outside of the house.

A secret passage. A way in — and a way out!

6

A Scrap of Paper

Bill was up and dressed at dawn. His mind had clarified while he dozed. He realized that he ought not to have spent the night in the mansion. He must find other lodgings that day, unless he was arrested as a material witness. But he rather imagined that Sims meant to play a waiting game. And he would come back secretly after he had obtained other accommodation, and try to discover what he was convinced was the secret entrance to the house.

He gathered his things together, and then, realizing that he was hungry, went into the kitchen, where he found some stale bread, and some cold meat in the icebox. Then he went out. He had a good deal to do that day; but first and foremost he must see Elsie. It seemed a year since they had been together.

As he left the front door, he saw a man turn into Spumetti's tonsorial parlor across the way, and he knew that he was still under surveillance. He bent his head to avoid the force of the wind, and the thin, pelting rain that was driving across the bluffs.

And that was how he happened to see something lying in the road, just outside the entrance to the yard. Bill stopped dead at the sight of it, though this was instinct, or the promptings of the unconscious, rather than reason. Then he picked it up.

It was a little scrap of paper, charred at the edges, lying against the root of one of the maples. It could have come from nowhere but the furnace. There was writing on it, just a few words in pencil, rain-soaked and almost undecipherable.

Bill glanced hastily across the street. The watcher was not in sight. Very carefully Bill held the charred fragment in his hand and made his way toward the steps that ran down to State Street.

They descended the face of the bluff vertically. Great rocks rose on either side of them. There were six flights of them, and at every second stage stood a light standard. It was not until Bill reached the bottom, and stood in an empty lot at the head of State Street, near the lunch wagon, that he looked at the piece of paper.

There were just four words, and it took quite some time to decipher them:

Eggleston — two miles — river.

Bill put the tiny scrap of charred paper inside his billfold. He knew where Eggleston was. It was a small town up the St. Croix, a river that divides the State of Maine from the Canadian province of New Brunswick. Bill felt that he was on the track at last.

He made his way to police headquarters. Emery had not arrived, but the first words of the sergeant at the desk depressed Bill much more than the discovery of the paper had elated him.

'Miss Garry ain't here,' said the sergeant. 'She was removed to the state prison at Thomaston last night, under an order for a change of venue.'

Bill stared at the sergeant, stunned.

'Can I see her, if I go there?' he asked.

'I guess you could get an order,' said the sergeant, sympathetically. 'But you'd best wait and see the Chief. In fact, he's just sent out a man to bring you in.'

'You mean I'm under arrest?'

'Nope, the Chief just wants to talk to you, as far as I know. I guess you know what happened last night.'

'I don't get you,' said Bill.

'You don't know Mr. Van Houten fell down the steps and broke his neck?'

'You mean he's dead?'

'Dead as he'll ever be. The Chief wants to see you about it.'

Bill sat down in a daze. Van Houten's death seemed to rob him of all hopes of proving Elsie's innocence — unless the Eggleston clue proved of value. Was it Van Houten who had escaped through the furnace the night before?

Emery came in in a few minutes.

'Glad to see you,' he nodded to Bill. 'Come inside. I want to talk to you about something.'

In the inner room, he waved Bill to a seat. 'What do you know about Mr. Van Houten's death?' he asked.

'I only heard about it from the sergeant five minutes ago,' said Bill.

'When did you see him last?'

'Yesterday afternoon, at the house. He was packing up his things. I saw him carry them out to his car. Then he drove away.'

'You slept at the house last night, Forrest. Why?' Emery drew out a cigar, bit the end off it, and began to chew; he forgot to light it.

'Well, my things were there, and I hadn't time to make other arrangements. Anything suspicious about that?' Bill demanded.

'Not one solitary thing. Looks to me, Forrest, as if you're doing your damnedest to get yourself in Dutch and can't succeed. So far as can be ascertained, Mr. Van Houten just lost his footing and fell down the rocks. His neck was broken, but there were no signs of violence upon him. I know you're all right, Forrest. I reckon you were badly hit by what happened yesterday. You say you saw Van Houten at the house. How did he seem? Nervous?'

'Near a breakdown, and pretty well shot with whisky.'

'Doctor Johnson found his stomach and brain pretty well loaded with alcohol. That's what makes it pretty certain it was an accident. But you say you saw him drive away. Then how in thunder did he happen to fall down the steps? He must have gone back for something. Did he go back?'

'I didn't see him, if he did. But the night was pretty stormy. He might have come in at the side door for something, and I wouldn't have heard him.'

'He left his car in Canns garage, and engaged a room at the Martin House,' said Emery. 'He must have gone back. You made a mistake in returning to the house, Forrest. I'd advise you to get other lodgings tonight. As a matter of fact, but for Doctor Johnson's report, you'd have had a lot of explaining to do — in jail.

'I know you're all right, and I told Sims so. In fact, we had quite a few words about you. Then he got that change of venue order from Judge Crosby at his summer place out at Atlantic, and took Miss Garry off to Thomaston.'

'Can I get an order to see her there?' asked Bill.

'No, you'll have to stay in town for the present, till I hear from Sims.' Emery rose. 'Pull yourself together, Forrest,' he said. 'Elsie Garry is as nice a little girl as I've ever known. She'll get off light. All you've got to do is to stay quiet. Move right away, and call me up when you've done so. And above everything else, keep quiet.'

He stretched out his hand and grasped Bill's warmly. 'I'd give — well, a month's pay if this hadn't happened,' he said. 'I hear you're retaining Hickson. If you want to see him, you'll probably find him in the police court.'

Bill left the office, passed through the outer room, and went up the stairs that led to the courtroom. He saw Hickson immediately. The lawyer was engaged in defending a petty offender, the red-faced man whom Bill had seen in his office the day before. Sims' assistant, a young fellow named Smart, was asking the Judge for a jail sentence, and Hickson was opposing.

'If he gets that fellow off, he'll get Elsie off,' Bill said to himself.

And Hickson did. When the man was released on payment of a fine of a hundred dollars, Bill's spirits rose once more. Hickson was certainly on the job.

The case concluded, Hickson turned away, then saw Bill. He nodded.

'Want to walk back to my office with me?' he asked. 'I've got an appointment in three-quarters of an hour, but I guess that will leave us plenty time to talk.'

Bill accompanied the lawyer out of the station.

They proceeded side by side in silence, until they had entered Hickson's office and closed the door. Hickson motioned Bill to a seat, stared at him, and began to drum his fingers again.

'Too bad about Mr. Van Houten,' he began. 'I guess you've heard?'

'Yeah, Emery sent for me, to ask me what I knew about it. I didn't quite get what he was driving at, since he said that Doctor Johnson certified it was an accident. Never mind Van Houten. You didn't see Miss Garry before they took her away?'

'No, Sims put it over on us,' answered the lawyer. 'I guess it won't hurt Miss Garry any, though, or help him. Now, what do you want me to do about it?'

'Stay on the case,' said Bill. 'I want you, and I don't want anybody else. Where's the trial going to be held?'

'In Thomaston, I should think. Do you want me to go up there and see Miss Garry?'

'I want you to go up as soon as possible. Can you see her today?'

'I might be able to run up this afternoon,' said Hickson. 'I'll be very glad to defend Miss Garry, if we can come to an agreement as to the line of defense. No need to go into that at present. As a matter of fact, this is going to be one of the biggest fights that have been staged. The lost Starr fortune makes it one of the biggest things in years. I'm interested in the girl, too. Professionally, it will mean a lot to me if I can secure a compromise verdict.'

'Damn a compromise verdict!' Bill

snorted. 'You're going to get an acquittal!'

Hickson drummed his fingers on the desk. 'Forrest, what's on your mind?' he asked. 'You were obviously too upset yesterday for me to go into details with you. Have you any ground for seriously believing that Elsie Garry is innocent?'

'I'm absolutely sure of it,' said Bill. 'Elsie Garry wouldn't have murdered her cousin over a piece of trumpery jewelry.'

'Who else could have stabbed Jenny Starr?'

There was something so skeptical about the lawyer's manner that Bill resolved then and there to tell him nothing, either about the intruder of the night before, or about the paper he had found. Not, at least, until he had followed up his own clues.

'I believe Van Houten was murdered,' said Bill. 'I believe the man who killed Van Houten stabbed Jenny Starr. I believe the cause had something to do with Abbie Starr's missing fortune. I'll tell you this much: a man named Jones, of Boston, is dickering for the purchase of the mansion. I saw him in the bank. I overheard his talk with the president. He was obviously bent on securing the property. Now, suppose Van Houten and Jenny Starr had got some clue to the disposition of those missing securities?'

'I can't follow you there, Forrest. However, it might be worthwhile following up this Jones clue. I'll see to it. I can get the information from the bank. You stay out of it. What does Jones look like?'

'Shortish, middle-aged man. I'd know him in a minute. He offered considerably more than the house is worth, under present conditions.'

A knock came at the door, a yell of 'Paper!' A boy appeared with an extra issue of the local morning sheet. Hickson took it, glanced at it, handed it to Bill, who glanced at the headlines.

It announced Van Houten's death, and also stated that a warrant was out for the arrest of the missing witness, Emily Bennett.

'Well, what d'you make of this?' asked Bill, pointing to the line in heavy type.

'Ran away because she was afraid, I'd say,' said the lawyer. 'She'll probably surrender today or tomorrow. I don't make much of that.

'Now see here, Forrest,' Hickson went on, 'I don't want you to think me a pessimist. To be frank, at present Elsie Garry hasn't the ghost of a chance of anything but a manslaughter verdict. However, I'll go up to Thomaston tonight and have a talk with her. And I'll follow up that matter of the man Jones you've spoken about. It's possible, just possible, that Elsie Garry is innocent.

'Now let me tell you something. There's another figure in the picture, and that's yourself. I happen to know that Sims left orders you were to be kept under close observation.'

'There was a flatfoot opposite the house all night,' admitted Bill. 'I don't see what Sims hopes to pin on me though.'

'Sims,' said Hickson, 'is out to make a reputation in one of the biggest murder cases that have come his way, and he has political ambitions. Don't think you're the only person who's working from an odd angle, Forrest. Nothing would gratify Sims more than to bring in the missing

Starr fortune as an incentive to the murder. Now maybe you begin to see why they're watching you, and hoping to get you to tie the rope round your own neck.'

'Yeah. I see that,' said Bill.

'Don't go back to that house.'

'I've got to get my things.'

'Get them quickly, then, and move. Get back to your job at the bank, and for the Lord's sake, don't compromise yourself by trying any amateur detective work. You're up against experts.'

'Emery advised me along the same lines. Old Emery's a square-shooter.'

He is. But remember, Forrest, in a case like this, every man jack is working for his own reputation, and not to help the other fellow. If Emery thought it was to his interest, he'd go the limit to stretch your neck in a noose. I'll see you the day after tomorrow, after I've been up to Thomaston. Then we'll decide whether or not you're going to want me.'

7

A Hunch and a Jam

The First National Bank of Martinfield is an imposing new building with white Corinthian pillars in front of it, and stands on the new avenue that is crossed by the Plough River bridge. Bill got there a little before noon.

Bill was one of the assistant tellers, but, since he was efficient, and not averse to work, a good deal of it naturally gravitated into his hands. Of late he had been engaged in cataloging and sorting a variety of miscellaneous documents that were being transferred from the safety-deposit vault downstairs to the records department. None of these was of any immediate importance, and they were taking up room that was needed.

Langley, the teller in the end cage, looked up and nodded as Bill entered. In view of the rumors about Bill that were circulating through Martinfield, he preferred to convey unspoken sympathy rather than to risk any tactless remark.

Bill went to the table in the rear, where he had been working, took off his coat and hung it on a nail, putting on his alpaca office coat instead. He found Higgins, who was in charge of the safety-deposit vault, went down with him and brought back a file of papers. These, consisted in the main of old deeds, cancelled notes and so forth, dating back for years.

Among them were a number that bore Abbie Starr's signature. Abbie Starr had at one time purchased securities, through the bank, and these particular papers consisted mostly of receipts. Bill studied them closely. The purchases had been of sound bonds, and considerable sums of money had been invested. The old woman had shown a good deal of shrewdness; there were records of considerable profits. Although the securities had decreased considerably in value, if Abbie had held on to them, she might have had the nucleus of a sizable fortune.

However, there was nothing to be learned from these. They had all been gone over after the old woman's death. If Van Houten had been guilty of defalcations or frauds, he had covered up his tracks quite ably.

Bill finished his work in about an hour, then tied up the papers again and went back to the vault with Higgins. Then he made his way to the president's office.

'Hello, Forrest,' said Doremus, looking up. He shook hands with Bill, as a mark of sympathy.

'I've got to ask you for a few days' leave of absence,' said Bill. 'I guess you'll understand. I don't feel able to get on the job till this matter steadies down.'

'Why — why, I guess, under the circumstances that's the best thing you can do,' Doremus answered. 'Terrible happenings! Poor Van Houten! I wish you the best of luck, Forrest.' He shook hands again.

Bill thanked him, went back and changed his coat. He saw Doctor Johnson cashing a check at Langley's cage, but Johnson didn't see him, and Bill waited until the doctor had gone before leaving the bank. It was not until he was in the street that he realized that Doremus had spoken as if he was not coming back any more.

'It sure looks as though they're figuring on my being arrested,' Bill said to himself.

He went to the railroad station and procured a timetable, which he studied in the waiting room. He was torn between the desire to go to Thomaston to try to see Elsie, and the impulse to go to Eggleston and try to solve the mystery of the scrap of writing. The successful solution was long odds, but Bill felt certain that the charred fragment was what was left of Jenny Starr's letter.

There was a train for Thomaston at four and another at seven in the evening, and there was a slow local that left for Eggleston at eight at night, meandering up through Maine, and making connection with the Canadian express at Houlton.

Before deciding on his destination, however, Bill had to move, and he set about finding new quarters. Two land-ladies in succession, who had promising rooms, stiffened when he revealed his identity to them, and backed out of the bargain. The third, a French Canadian woman, didn't seem to know who he was, and eagerly rented the large room at the rear of the ground floor.

Bill took a taxi up to the manor, got his things and moved in. Then he called up police headquarters and informed them of his new address. Then he went to a lunch wagon for dinner.

At 7:30 he made his way by a devious route toward the railroad station. After he had satisfied himself that he was not being followed, he mingled with the throngs on Main Street. He felt more and more strongly that Eggleston was the right destination for him that night.

He slipped into the station among the crowds. A train for Portland was leaving a few minutes before the one for Eggleston and the station, was jammed. Bill bought his ticket and felt sure that the clerk had failed to recognize him. He crossed the tracks to the Eggleston train, and ensconced himself in the empty smoking compartment.

The Portland train pulled out along the tracks beside him. A couple of men came into the smoking compartment, but they were strangers, and gave him only a casual glance as they moved on to a seat at the end of the coach. The compartment was full of stale smoke, and Bill had a headache. His nerves were tense, too. If he had been recognized and followed, he would certainly be arrested for attempting to leave town.

It was with a sensation of intense relief that he finally felt the train glide out of the station. Satisfied that he had made his getaway unobserved, he relaxed and lit a cigarette.

He smoked one cigarette after another. The train stopped at three or four way-stations during the first hour. Another man dropped into the smoker and the two who had got on at Martinfield left. There was now only one stop before Eggleston, and that was at Riverport, a town of about five thousand inhabitants, on the bank of the St. Croix.

Bill could see the broad river extended before him, the moonlight rippling on its surface. Across was the Canadian province of New Brunswick. The country was a waste of sawed-over lumber land. Presently the train began to slow down. A huddle of lights appeared. This was the last stop before Eggleston, Riverport, and no more than ten miles from Bill's destination.

Bill felt himself growing more and more nervous. He lit another cigarette. He went to the ice-water container near the wash room and poured himself a drink of tepid water. From the window he could see only some half dozen persons on the platform.

The train got under way again. Bill went back to his seat.

Another passenger came into the smoking compartment. He was a tall, rawboned, farmer-looking person, of about forty years, and as he passed Bill he gave him a keen glance from beneath his shapeless hat. He hesitated.

'Mind if I sit down by you?' he asked,

Bill glanced at the long rows of empty

seats, then shrugged his shoulders.

'The train is yours,' he said.

'Much obliged, friend.' The man sat down, then half turned in his seat and surveyed Bill as if he were a horse, checking him up.

'Your name William Forrest?' he asked.

Bill felt himself grow hot, then cold. 'I don't just recall where I've seen *your face* before,' he said, as insultingly as possible.

'Blue-gray eyes, light hair, and wearing either a blue serge or a pin-stripe. That suit you've got on is a pin-stripe, Mister. Soft hands. And you'd stand about five feet ten, wouldn't you?' asked the stranger insinuatingly.

'*Go on and get it over,*' snapped Bill.

The stranger eyed him with an appraising stare. Bill stared back.

'*Get it over!*' he snapped. 'What is it you want?'

'Now take it gently. You ain't in a bad jam; there ain't no criminal charge against you.' He drew back the lapel of his coat and displayed a star. 'I'm Sheriff Prouty, of this county. Got a wire from police headquarters, at Martinfield, to see if you was on this train. You're wanted as a material and absconding witness in the Jenny Starr murder case. We get off at Eggleston, and I'm holding you there over night, until they come for you.'

'*The hell you are!*' said Bill.

'Now don't take it that way,' said the sheriff. 'You ain't in bad at all. Have a cigar.'

But it wasn't a cigar that Sheriff Prouty was feeling for. Even country sheriffs don't carry cigars in their coat side-pockets. The sheriff had seen the bad glint in Bill's eyes, and what Bill saw emerging from the pocket was the edge of a steel handcuff.

'*I'm* taking it this way,' said Bill, in an access of sudden desperation, and swung his arm sidewise.

Sheriff Prouty was surprisingly quick. There came the flash of the handcuffs; but the sheriff's movement wasn't quite quick enough. Before he knew where he was, he was sprawling on the floor, and Bill was on his feet and speeding along the aisle of the compartment.

The slow local was pulling up an incline at a speed of about fifteen miles an hour. Bill gained the vestibule, glanced back and saw the sheriff rising to his feet. He looked down at the cindery track beneath him, hesitated a bare fraction of a second, and then launched himself into space.

8

The House of Death

He struck the track squarely upon his shoulders, rolled over and felt the painful impact of cinders upon his nose and forehead. He rolled down the incline into a jungle of scrub pine. He leaped to his feet, and raced forward into the young growth of the cut-over forest.

Behind him he could hear the sheriff yelling. He saw a cluster of passengers gathering in the vestibule of the car that adjoined the smoker, and heard the screech of the brakes being applied to the engine. He saw the five-car train being pulled to a standstill. He saw a figure leap to the ground, followed by others, and knew that the indomitable sheriff was in pursuit.

He ran on. He was effectively concealed from the view of his pursuers by the dense undergrowth that grew along the side of the track, and, in spite of the moonlight, he knew that it would be easy to avoid capture. He struck out a trail through the trees until he reached another clump of undergrowth; then he just sat down and waited.

He could not see the searching party, but he heard them calling to one another some distance away. He guessed that Sheriff Prouty wasn't going to spend the night looking for a needle in a haystack, and even the slow local wasn't going to wait more than a few minutes. Sure enough, within five minutes of the time of his leap from the train, he saw it begin to move along the rails again. It rounded a bend and disappeared from sight.

For the present Bill was safe. His pursuers were all aboard. As soon as the train reached Eggleston, Sheriff Prouty would doubtless start burning up the wires in all directions, but Eggleston itself was the last place where Bill would be expected, unless the police had traced his destination from the booking clerk. Most probably they would be looking for him at Houlton, expecting that he would try to board the Canadian express.

Bill got up and stretched his limbs. He picked a few cinders out of his forehead and rubbed away the blood. He started off through the trees in the direction of the river, and pretty soon came in sight of it, stretching away in front of him, parallel with the railroad track.

Then he came to a tarred road running alongside it. He guessed there would be no danger till he reached Eggleston. He trudged on steadily.

About two miles from the town, he passed a farm house, and paused to consider whether it was worthwhile making investigations there. He decided that it wasn't. The farm house was not near the river, and the scrap of paper had mentioned the word river.

Eggleston came into Bill's ken suddenly, crossroads with a yellow traffic light above, motor cars, young people from summer camps and hotels strolling about the streets, boys in whites, girls in beach pajamas. Nobody paid any attention to Bill, not even the policeman who stood at the entrance to the cross-roads grocery store, chatting with the proprietor.

A little farther on was the police station. A sergeant sat behind the desk, reading a magazine, a cigar drooping from the corner of his mouth. A police officer lolled in a chair, talking to a man in civilian clothes. No signs of excitement there. Bill just glanced in and continued on his way.

A little farther still, the electric lights in front of a building proclaimed it to be the Eggleston Arms. Bill glanced in as he passed. Then his real shock came. He saw Sheriff Prouty standing in the lobby, surrounded by an interested group, to whom he was detailing what doubtless was his version of his battle with the desperado.

Bill passed the hotel quickly, and was glad when he found himself on the river road again, with the lights of the town behind him. He sauntered on, until the whir of a car, coming on swiftly from behind, made him leap aside.

That car was being driven at the rate of something like sixty miles an hour. It was a coupé and it contained a single occupant, a man. With body hunched over the steering-wheel and eyes fixed on the road ahead of him, the driver seemed entirely regardless of the pedestrian whom he had nearly run down. But Bill recognized the driver. He was a middle-aged man, with a clipped beard and a high forehead showing under his pushed back hat.

It was Doctor Johnson, the coroner at Martinfield!

Bill stood stock still until the tail light of the car had disappeared in the distance. Then he went on. He was staggered by Johnson's appearance in Eggleston. That the doctor's presence had some bearing upon his own quest, Bill did not doubt for a moment. It was quite unbelievable that mere chance had brought Johnson to the same town, thirty-five miles from Martinfield.

But what was he doing there? It was no part of a coroner's task to engage in the hue and cry after an escaped witness. Bill only knew that he was going to follow that coupé, and he went on doggedly, scanning the road carefully.

The string of small houses outside the town had given place to forest again. Bill continued on his way until he estimated that he was fully three miles from Eggleston. The paper scrap had said two, but there were no signs of a house or camp, nothing but the second growth, extending down to the St. Croix, of which Bill got occasional glimpses in the moonlight. Only on the Canadian side of the river did an occasional light gleam from a farm house. As there was no bridge hereabouts, the quest couldn't end on the Canadian side.

Just as Bill was beginning to wonder how much farther he would have to go, he saw the lights of a house shining through the trees beside the water.

There were several lights in the house, which stood back in a grove of trees, with the river almost at the back door. A picket fence, forming what looked like a large enclosure, and continuing to an open gate and a driveway. The light was on above the entrance of the house, and Bill could see Doctor Johnson's coupé standing in front of it.

And with that Bill knew that he had reached the end of his objective. He crouched among the trees that overhung the picket fence and looked inside.

The lights, he now discovered, came from the rooms on the upper floor. Except for the light over the entrance, the ground floor was dark. Bill retraced his steps for a few yards and found a gap in the picket fence, which was old and sagging. He squeezed through and made his way softly forward.

He could now distinguish the outlines of the house. It was of two stories, long and rambling, and had evidently been a farm house at some period. For the matter of that, it might be a farm house still. The light over the door was not reflected from the vestibule, which showed that the house, like the picket fence, was in need of paint.

As Bill stopped for a moment at the edge of the grove of trees through which he was advancing, the light above the doorway went out. Bill went forward again upon the side of the house that was in the moon-shadow. He could see silhouettes passing and repassing against the drawn shade of one of the upper windows. He thought he heard the sound of voices, several voices, engaged in animated discussion.

He moved round to the rear of the house. A window loomed up darkly in front of him. Bill pressed his fingertips against the sides of it and found that it was un-hasped. Very softly he began pushing the window upward, until there was an opening large enough for him to climb through.

He listened. He could hear the murmur of voices upstairs. A woman's voice rose high in expostulation and was instantly suppressed. Bill squeezed through the open window and dropped upon the floor with in. The room in which he was was pitch-dark.

He struck a match and discovered that he was in a kitchen. At the end of it was a closed door. Bill reached that door by the last flicker of his match and softly opened it.

At once he could hear the angry chatter of the voices above. Then a door slammed on the upper story, and the sounds were cut off. But a light came down the stairs from another room, apparently, and by its aid Bill could see a stretch of hall, and the stairs looming darkly beyond. He crossed the hall, which was heavily carpeted.

Suddenly a scream rang out from inside the room with the closed door. A scream, followed by another, then a shot. A man's oath, and the sound of a body thudding upon the floor and reverberating through the house. Then utter silence.

That silence, following the outcry, was more gruesome than the screams and the shot. Bill leaped up the stairs.

The light shone from a large and apparently empty room on the upper story. There was another light in another room. Both these doors were open. But the room from which the sounds had come was at the end of the upper hall, and the door was closed.

Bill could hear the scuffling of feet and voices whispering frantically. He flung himself against the door. It gave. A woman stood in the entrance, facing him with fear-twisted face — the missing nurse, Emily Bennett!

The room was very large. There was a

door opposite opening either upon a cupboard or upon a flight of back stairs, and a man was thrusting some heavily wrapped human figure through the doorway. And on the floor lay the body of Doctor Johnson, extended on its side, and motionless.

A pear-shaped stream of blood, issuing from one temple, formed a widening pool upon the carpet.

Mrs. Bennett screamed out Bill's name, fought him, tried to impede his entrance.

He pushed her aside and forced his way into the room. The man who had pushed the third figure through the doorway slammed the door and turned. He swung round, gun in hand, and fired. The bullet whizzed past Bill's ear.

Before the man could fire again, Bill closed with him, grappling for the gun. He had recognized his assailant. It was Jones, the man who had been dickering with the bank for the purchase of the Starr mansion.

Jones yelled with rage, and fought with all his might to free his right hand from Bill's grasp. Short though he was, he was of tremendous strength, and it was all Bill could do to keep his fingers clamped about the wrist of the gun-hand.

With their free hands they buffeted each other's faces, they reeled to and fro about the room.

'Hold him!' Jones shouted to Emily Bennett. 'Knock him out! Damn you, can't you do *anything*?'

Bill succeeded in sending a straight left into Jones' face that sent him staggering backward. But still gripping Jones' wrist, he himself was thrown off his stance by the other's sudden recoil. Then, with a screech, Emily Bennett leaped at Bill from behind, swinging an uplifted chair.

She struck at Bill's head with all her force. The bottom rung of the chair caught Bill's neck at the back, just above the collar, and the shock almost dislocated one of his vertebrae.

As he staggered under the shock, Jones succeeded in wrenching his right hand free. He swept the gun up wildly and fired again. But the aim was too rapid. Bill escaped death by fully an inch, but the powder stung his face and eyes, partly blinding him. The bullet struck the chair as it dropped.

Jones pressed the trigger once more, but this time it only clicked on a spent cartridge. Bill leaped. He was too slow. Jones swung the weapon, and the muzzle caught Bill over the right ear. Instantly the room became ablaze with brilliant lights. They moved like meteors out of a void of encompassing darkness.

Bill felt his knees sagging under him. He saw dimly the leering face of Jones above him, alight with triumph. He tried to gather himself together, and struck out with his fist, but Jones swung his head and the blow glanced past his face harmlessly. And before Bill could make another movement, Emily Bennett had him pinioned from behind.

'Knock him out!' hissed the woman. 'Give him a real one! He's going now!'

Again the revolver swung, and a second time it dropped upon Bill's head. Bill was not conscious of any pain, but his knees buckled, and he felt himself going down. The faces of Jones and Mrs. Bennett faded out of his consciousness. The whirl of meteoric lights went out in complete blackness.

Bill dropped unconscious to the floor, by the side of the dead coroner.

9

Escape

It was only for a few moments that Bill was entirely out of the picture. With a tremendous effort of will, he succeeded in pulling himself up from the depths of darkness. He lay upon the floor, apparently inert, and yet he was, in a way, aware of what was taking place, as if he saw it as a spectator at a play.

Jones had recharged his revolver and was placing it to Bill's head: Emily Bennett caught his arm. 'No! That's not the way!' she cried.

'He's got to go, I tell you. God knows how he got on the job, but he knows more than anybody's got the right to.'

'Not that way, Louis! Listen!'

She began talking swiftly, while Jones listened, and gradually the hand that was aiming the gun at Bill's head drooped.

'That's clever,' Jones said, at last. 'You

always were a clever one, Emily. But will it work?'

'It's *got* to work. There's a warrant out for his arrest as an absconding witness. It came over the radio while I was downstairs. I told you so.'

'Yeah, but how about yourself?'

'No one will know me. I've made my reputation in Eggleston. I'm the last person they would suspect. It will work like a charm, don't you see? *He killed the doctor.*'

'Lord, Emily, it's a fool-proof alibi!' exclaimed Jones, in admiration. 'Can you work it alone, while I get that old drugged carcass back to Martinfield?'

'Of course I can. Have I ever left you holding the bag yet?' answered Emily Bennett. 'Get on your way quick. He'll be expecting you!'

'Let's take a look at this fellow first,' said Jones.

He bent over Bill, who lay as still as if entirely unconscious. Jones prodded him in the side with his toe, looked at the lumps on his head, with the blood trickling from them.

'He's out for hours,' he said, straightening himself. 'You sure have got a head, Emily! Remember, he broke into the house and pulled a gun on the doctor. The doctor snatched up that chair and hit him on the head with it. Then this fellow shot the doctor dead. Wait!'

He picked up the gun, which still lay on the floor, and, wiping it clean upon his coat, took Bill's hand and impressed fingers and thumb-print on it. Then he smeared the leg and rung of the chair in the pool of blood that was seeping into the carpet.

'All right,' he said. 'Lock the door on the outside and phone Sheriff Prouty. Tell him to get here as quick as he can. You'd best be hiding somewhere outside the house when he arrives. And don't forget to let out a yell or two.'

He went to the cupboard opposite the door and picked up the shrouded figure that he had hidden there. It lay limp and apparently lifeless in his arms. Staggering slightly under his burden, he made his way down the stairs.

Emily Bennett, after casting a final

101

glance at Bill's motionless body, followed him. The door closed, and there came the click of the lock as the key was turned.

'Lemme get a few minutes' start, before you call up Prouty,' said Jones at the front hall, resting his burden for a moment on the floor. 'See you soon, Emily. You've played trumps all through.'

He picked up his burden again and carried it to Johnson's car, where he deposited it in the seat on the right-hand side, setting it in position artistically, so that, whether or not it was ever likely to come to life again, it would look sufficiently living to anyone who passed in another car. Emily Bennett followed him.

'All okay, Louis?' she asked.

There was real affection in the kiss that the strange couple exchanged. Emily Bennett waited until the car had chugged away — two or three minutes, perhaps — then she crept softly up the stairs and listened at the door of the room. Not a sound came from it. Bill's wits were still wool-gathering.

She had not the courage to go back into that room of death. Satisfied that Bill was still out, she crept downstairs to phone.

'Central, I want police headquarters at once,' she cried in agitated tones. 'Something terrible has happened. Give me the sheriff!'

A moment later the crisp voice of the police officer on duty came to her ears.

'This is Mrs. Leibman at the sanatorium out on the Houlton Road,' whimpered the woman. 'Oh, it's so terrible! Doctor Johnson, the Martinfield coroner, has been *murdered*!'

'Murdered! Who killed him?'

'I don't know. A young man who answered to the description of that escaped criminal you broadcast about earlier this evening. He broke into the house with a gun and shot the doctor, who'd just arrived to see a dying patient. The doctor just had time to snatch up a chair and knock him senseless before he was killed.'

'Where's the man?' snapped the police officer.

'He's lying in the bedroom, still senseless. Maybe he's dead. I locked the door. I'm afraid to stay in the house. Can you send the sheriff out right away, before he recovers consciousness? I — I'll be somewhere in the grounds, waiting for him. I'm afraid to stay in the house.'

'You stay around the place somewhere. We'll have the sheriff out in a few minutes,' the police officer said.

Of what was taking place downstairs, Bill had no glimmering, but he had heard the car drive away, and now he knew — knew that the solution of the mystery was almost at his fingertips, if he could pull himself out of that deathly torpor that gripped him.

He knew that, unless he could make a safe getaway to Martinfield and follow up his clue, not only he, but Elsie, must inevitably face the death sentence. The case against both of them would be iron-clad.

And it was the picture of Elsie, in her cell at Thomaston, that enabled Bill to make the final effort that pulled him back to life and vitality.

He got upon his knees, upon his feet. He tottered, staring down at the face of the dead coroner beside him. He fought off the swirls of blackness that were still creeping up. He bent and went through the dead man's pockets.

There was nothing in them. Whatever had been in them had doubtless been removed by Jones.

Bill tottered to the door. He had been faintly aware of the clicking lock. He tried it softly. Yes, it was locked. No use trying to break out that way.

He went to the door on the opposite side of the room. It led only into a closet, a large closet, in which a number of old-fashioned clothes, women's clothes, were hanging.

He went to the window. The drop to the ground was a dangerous one, but there was a Virginia creeper growing up the wall, a creeper with strong branches. The moon had shifted sufficiently to throw a light upon that side of the house.

Bill quietly unlatched the window, and softly threw it up. He flung his leg over the window sill, seated himself upon the edge, then slipped downward and felt for the vine. His foot came in contact with one of the main branches, and next moment, clinging to the stout tendrils, he was making his descent toward the ground.

But before he reached the ground he heard the swift purring of a car coming along the road. As he stepped down, he heard it stop in front of the driveway.

Bill glanced round the house. Everything was in moonlight now, and there was an open space of twenty-five yards between the house and the nearest trees. No possibility of darting to the safety of the forest without being spotted.

He crept cautiously around the edge of the building, and peered out. He saw the redoubtable Sheriff Prouty and two police officers hurrying up the drive. At the same moment the figure of Emily Bennett went running along the path toward them.

'Oh, thank God you're here, Sheriff!' Bill heard her cry. 'He's up there. You must be careful, he's a desperate man. He shot poor Doctor Johnson down in cold blood.'

'We'll take care of him,' rasped the sheriff, pulling a revolver from the holster at his belt. 'Is he in the room with the patient?'

'No, my husband started for Martinfield with her just before the doctor arrived. He didn't understand that he was coming, and her case was almost hopeless. He's alone up there. But he's desperate, I tell you.'

'Don't worry,' said Sheriff Prouty.

As the four figures disappeared within the house, Bill slipped out of the narrow edging of shadow and backed toward the grove of trees. He reached them undetected. But, once there, he was forced to stop. He was still groggy from the blows that he had received.

He heard the sheriff and the officers running up the stairs, their steps sounding thunderous in the stillness.

The sound of the shattered door crashed through the night. Yells of rage indicated that his escape had been discovered.

There followed the rush down the stairs again.

Bill pulled himself together. He was himself once more, save for his badly aching head. He was halfway between the house and the sheriff's car, parked in front of the drive. He saw his means of making his getaway to Martinfield — if the sheriff had left his key in the ignition.

No time to hesitate, it was now or never. Even as he turned, the door of the house opened, and the three men came into view, with Emily Bennett in the background.

'Round the back! Round the back!' Bill heard Prouty yelling. 'Scatter and search them trees. Shoot him, if he won't surrender.'

It certainly was now or never. Bill turned and sprinted across the open toward the sheriff's car.

He was seen before he had covered a quarter of the distance. A yell from the sheriff was echoed by the two police officers.

'Stop, or I'll fire!' cried Prouty.

Bill raced on. There followed the crack of the sheriff's gun. But Bill was running in the shadow cast by the grove of trees, and the distance was a little too great for accurate aiming. The bullet whistled a foot to one side of Bill's face.

'Let him have it!' cried Prouty, and again opened fire, the police officers joining in. The slugs hooted about Bill's ears. One of them crashed into the gateway just as Bill reached it, and his hand dropped upon the splintered wood. Then Bill had cleared the entrance and leaped into the car through the opened doorway. He gave a cry of exultation. The sheriff *had* left his key in the ignition!

Bill turned the key in the ignition, pressed his foot upon the starter. The sheriff and the two officers were halfway to the gate now, and firing as they ran. The glass on Bill's left hand dissolved in a shower of fragments. *Clang, clang*, went the slugs as they pierced the hood. Behind the three, Mrs. Bennett stood, sending up shrieks of affected terror.

The engine caught. Bill flung the gear into second. The car began to move just as the sheriff, followed by his satellites, reached the gateway. Prouty took deliberate aim at Bill, who ducked just in time. The slug passed just where his head had been and starred the window on his right.

The car was moving fast. Bill swung

into high. A slug passed over his head and embedded itself in the roof. The picket fence was swinging by.

The yelling died away. At fifty miles an hour, Bill swung the dilapidated police car about and headed back toward Eggleston.

Five minutes later he reached a crossroads marked Eggleston and Martinfield, the latter town forty-five miles away. Bill turned onto the concrete highway. On his right he saw the lights of Eggleston, shining in the distance. He whizzed past them, then took a dirt road that ran back toward the river, and a few minutes later was heading back toward Martinfield, watching the stream of lights that followed one another along the parallel highway some half-mile to his left.

Eggleston was already on the job, searching for him.

10

The End of the Tunnel

Bill turned on his parking lights, turned them off again. Better to trust to speed, than try to make his way along that road in comparative darkness. He stepped hard on the gas, and saw the needle of the speedometer move up to fifty-five. That was as much as the sheriff's car seemed capable of making. As it was, the light car bumped and bounded over the gaps in the tarred surface, and two or three times Bill came perilously near disaster as he negotiated a sharp turn.

He came out on a better road. There was the flash of traffic moving in both directions, and he slowed down to forty. He felt fairly safe now, at least, until he reached the outskirts of Martinfield. And that was the last place that anyone would suspect that he was making for.

He struck a concrete road and let the

speedometer run up to fifty. He knew where he was now. Only one village between himself and Martinfield. He saw it, a straggle of lights, then a long street, empty in the moonlight. He passed a yellow beacon. A policeman, leaped out from somewhere and shouted at him. But the man was lost to sight in an instant, and Bill was through the village, and pounding along the right-hand arm of a forked road.

And now Bill was entering Martinfield, and again he dropped to forty. Jones, or Leibman, or whatever he called himself, couldn't be far ahead of him. Bill turned north out of Main Street, along the road that led to the winding street around the bluffs. There was only one traffic light in the way, and Bill could see the bluff looming up ahead of him. And the traffic light was set at yellow, for the night.

But as Bill passed it, a motorcycle policeman shot out of a side street, with a yell. He flung his cycle to one side of Bill's car, motioning to him to pull over. Bill shot up to the limit. The street ahead of him was empty.

The cop, crowded to one side of the road, fell back. There came the rapid discharge of four shots in succession. Bill's car lurched crazily. This time one of the rear tires had been blown out.

With a convulsive effort, Bill kept his control of the wheel. The car was slowing, but it was still traveling at fair speed, and Bill held it in the center of the road. The bluff was right in front of him, with a stretch of vacant lots at the foot, and only a few lights here and there. Bill turned his own lights out, opened the right-hand door, and leaped.

He landed on all fours beside the road, with a shock that jarred every bone in his body. But the motorcycle cop, speeding alongside again, hadn't been prepared for that maneuver. He couldn't stop in time. It was all he could do to avoid collision with the crazily careening car now running amuck.

It leaped the curb, slithered across the muck and through the weeds, and came to a standstill almost at the foot of the rocks. Before the motorcyclist could straighten himself out, Bill had regained his feet and had disappeared in a dark alley that loomed up beside him.

Having ascertained that no bones were broken, Bill halted at the end of the alley and turned his steps toward the bluff. He was not far from the head of State Street. He could see the winding road some distance to his left, and could hear the motorcycle cop blowing his whistle frantically for aid. On his right were the steps running up the face of the bluff. Bill decided to take a chance.

Nobody was in sight, the steps were unguarded. Bill began to ascend the flights, leaping up two steps at a time, his heart pounding in his chest, as he realized that he was almost at his destination. Underneath him he could see a knot of men gathered about the stalled car, and others scurrying to and fro, searching for him. He gained the summit, paused for a moment to get his breath, and saw the Starr mansion in its grove of trees. He laughed. He had thrown his pursuers off the track. In the next few minutes he would know!

He reached the entrance. A figure

stepped out from beneath one of the maples and presented a revolver at his chest. In the moonlight Bill recognized Detective Ralston.

'Hello, Forrest!' said Ralston, 'Put 'em up, *quick*! This is business. I sort of guessed you'd be back here.'

Bill sprang. His shoulder struck Ralston's right hand, and the shock snapped the trigger, but the slug whistled harmlessly over Bill's head. Bill's right connected with the detective's jaw with a force that sent him sprawling in the mud. In an instant Bill had leaped upon the prostrate man and snatched away his gun.

Leaving Ralston floundering in the mud, Bill ran to the front door of the house and hurled himself against it.

He dashed through into the kitchen and down the kitchen steps. The interior of the cellar was faintly illumined by the moonlight that came through one of the little windows. Bill flung the furnace door wide open, leaned in and tugged at the grate. It didn't come loose, as he had expected, but it went back on its hinges. Bill felt underneath. There was a slab of stone, and in the center of the slab was an iron ring.

Bill tugged with all his might. He felt the slab begin to move. Also, he heard Ralston in the house, running to and fro.

The slab gave with a heave that sent Bill's already much battered head back against the interior of the iron furnace.

Bill saw meteors all over again. He must have yelled, for he heard Ralston stop overhead and then make a rush for the kitchen stairs.

But Bill was already squeezing himself feet first into the hole beneath him, just wide enough for a man. Incredible that Jones, alias Leibman, had passed that way.

He dropped ten feet, feeling the rungs of a wooden ladder brush against him as he descended. He found himself standing in a tunnel, head-high, and just as wide as his body. He could hear Ralston above, in the cellar.

Bill began to grope his way along the tunnel. He had to stoop, to prevent his head from striking the roof. And the earth roof quickly gave place to stone. The walls on either side, which in places pressed closely against Bill's body, seemed to be of rammed earth, hard as rock. The tunnel sloped sharply; in one place Bill lost his footing and slid for a dozen feet and more before he was able to pull up.

He knew where he was then. He was over the edge of the bluffs and sliding down toward the streets of the town. Of a sudden, he saw a glimmer of light ahead of him. He went on a little more slowly, his eyes fixed upon it. Presently there was no doubt of it. It was — unbelievable though it might seem — an electric light. One? No, a cluster of them.

In front of him Bill could see what looked like an open doorway. He could hear the murmur of voices. Very cautiously now he proceeded, until he could see the door quite clearly. It had seemed on a level with his body, but actually it was overhead. It was a trap door, and the lights were shining overhead.

He could hear the voices clearly. He looked up, blinking into the brilliancy of the light cluster above him. He heard Jones-Leibman speaking.

'When she comes out of it she'll tell. By

God, we'll make her tell — shamming all this time, the old devil, and fooling all of us! The point is, you'll have to get her into the passage and keep her there till she squeals.'

'No difficulty about that,' answered a voice. 'We'll get her in at once. There's a hiding place that was excavated in the old days — '

'What's that?' cried Leibman, in alarm.

Bill leaped up through the opening. 'It's me,' he said. 'Throw up your hands, the pair of you! Your game's finished!'

He knew — he had known for certain all along, since he had gone through those old records in the bank. Yet it was like a dream, as he found himself standing at the edge of the trap door in Frank Hubbard's mortuary, with the circular stone walls, the loopholes, the two stone slabs, and the electric lights overhead.

Frank Hubbard and the man Leibman stood as if palsied as Bill leaped through the trap. Behind them, lying on one of the stone slabs, was the drugged form that Bill had seen in the sanatorium near Eggleston.

'Throw 'em up!' Bill repeated.

He had not calculated sufficiently upon the desperation of the two. Hubbard leaped upon him, and Bill's trigger clicked harmlessly. Ralston had gone to capture him with a gun that held a single shell.

Hubbard, fingers twined about Bill's throat, seemed utterly regardless of the jolts from Bill's fists that were rapidly reducing his lips to pulp.

'Shoot him! *Shoot him*, you fool!' snarled Hubbard, beside himself with fury.

Leibman was circling round the two, gun in hand, looking for his chance. It came. The roar of his revolver filled the mortuary. Bill felt a sudden shock in the side.

'Hold him!' screeched Hubbard, staggering forward. 'I'll give him a shot that will put him out of business!'

Bill was upon one knee. Leibman was gripping him, pounding him. Hubbard darted into the laboratory adjoining. Bill, helpless in Leibman's grasp, fought feebly.

With an oath Leibman hurled him to the stone floor, half stunning him. As Bill lay there, he saw Hubbard come running back, a syringe in his hand. There was a look of gloating satisfaction on the mortician's face.

'Hold him, Leibman,' he said. 'This acts quicker than greased lightning.'

'*Stay there!*' roared a voice from the trap door.

Bill's rolling eyes took in the figure of Detective Ralston. At the sight of him Hubbard leaped back and let the syringe fall. Then, with a yell, he bolted back into his funeral parlor.

The last thing that Bill heard was the click of the handcuffs on Leibman's wrists.

11

'Ante-Mortem'

It was eight days later. Sims and Emery were seated at Bill's bedside in the Martinfield hospital.

And it was a very chastened Sims. Gone was the blandness, the sort of sub-dued arrogance that had characterized him on the occasion of Bill's last interview with him.

'So this,' said Bill feebly, 'is what you call an ante-mortem.'

'Ante-mortem be damned!' said Emery. 'You're getting well just as quick as you can, Forrest. You'll be on your feet and out of here in another week. What I'm trying to get at is how you knew that Abbie Starr *hadn't* died, but had been kept a prisoner at that place at Eggleston for nearly two years.'

'It was those four penciled words on the piece of paper,' answered Bill. 'There was a curious loop to the t's that was quite characteristic. I was sure I had seen it before, so I looked up these old signatures of Abbie Starr's at the bank, and after that I hadn't very much doubt. Too bad she never regained consciousness.'

'Yes, Leibman had given her enough dope to kill an ox,' said Emery. 'She must have been dead long before he got her to the mortuary. And with her death, all chance of finding those securities seems to have gone, though as a matter of fact, I don't believe there were any.'

'My God, what a game to play!' said Sims.

Bill and the prosecuting attorney together with Emery, had pretty well pieced out the plot. It was Johnson, called in when the old woman was found lying unconscious on the kitchen floor, who had conceived the idea of a fake burial, and had spirited her away to the lonely farm house near Eggleston, in the hope of forcing her to divulge the secret of her fortune when she recovered from her stroke of paralysis.

To do that, he had had to take Hubbard

into his confidence. It was Hubbard who had become the dominating figure in the conspiracy, Hubbard who had engaged the Leibmans to take care of the house and the old, sick woman, while Johnson was filling his role of doctor and coroner in Martinfield.

'Abbie Starr had guts,' said Emery. 'She must have recovered her powers of speech and movement long ago. And she knew that if Johnson discovered it, he'd force her to talk. And that would be her finish. She lay there and waited till she got the chance to smuggle out that penciled note to Jenny Starr, asking for aid.

'The Leibmans found out about it, and Mrs. Leibman hurried down to Martinfield and got a room under the name of Bennett, hoping to intercept the letter before it was forwarded from Jenny Starr's former address. When she failed, poor Jenny Starr had to be rubbed out. But that tunnel — Lord, to think that Hubbard was prowling about all the while under the Starr mansion!'

'And then,' said Sims, 'as far as I can make out, Johnson got scared, and answered a posthaste summons to the Sanatorium, where Leibman, at Hubbard's orders, was to make away with him. Your arrival gave them just the chance they wanted to pin the murder on you. Leibman brought Abbie Starr back to make her talk, but he gave her too big a shot of dope. Hubbard and Leibman were the masterminds in the whole conspiracy. Johnson was a child in their hands.'

'Yeah, Johnson must have gone through hell,' said Emery, 'having Abbie Starr on his hands all that while, not daring to kill her, and not knowing that she was shamming after she recovered from her stroke. Well, Leibman and Hubbard are booked to dance at the rope's end.'

'And how soon will Miss Garry be set free?' asked Bill.

'Oh, you won't have so long to wait,' answered Emery, rising. He looked at Sims, and a smile spread across the chastened face of the prosecutor.

He nodded, and Bill relaxed himself upon the pillow. He closed his eyes. He opened them as a shadow fell across his bed. He stared up into Elsie's face.

'Oh Bill, Bill!' cried Elsie, falling upon her knees beside him. 'You're going to get well, Bill. The doctor just told me. They wouldn't let me come in before. They — they — '

Her arms went round Bill's neck, and Bill drew her face down to his chest. All the past was wiped out. Bill only knew that he was in a heaven of sleepy rapture.

'Elsie — '

'Bill, dear, they said you mustn't talk to me after seeing those two men. They said you've got to rest and get well again.'

'Yeah, that's all right,' said Bill. 'But — it's *still* September, isn't it?'

'It's September,' said Elsie, 'and then we'll have *every* month in the year together.'

Woman and the Law

1

Hollis stopped and threw another log on the fire, watching the flames shrivel the brittle bark, before leaning back in his chair again. He fixed his gaze upon the man on the other side of the fireplace.

'Do you mean what you said literally, Segrue?' he asked.

Judge Segrue exhaled a cloud of smoke from his cigar, and watched it curl upward until, caught by the heat of the fire, it dissolved in whirling rings. He pressed his slim fingertips together as he answered, with deliberate emphasis:

'Yes, Hollis, that is my *exact* opinion. Law is a very rough and ready instrument of justice. Often it is an instrument of injustice. The older I grow in experience, the more I become convinced that the ancient custom of private vengeance in specific cases is based on a correct human instinct.'

It was an astonishing thing for Judge

Segrue to have said. The Judge was the embodiment of all that was conservative and correct. Coming from anyone but himself, his remark would have appeared irresponsible. But for nearly forty years Segrue had been going from strength to strength in the estimation of his contemporaries. He leaned back, drawing at his cigar, and watching his auditors, a faintly ironical smile upon his handsome face.

He was speaking in the clubroom. But it was more like the living room of a private mansion. The fishing club was the organization of a few wealthy men who had purchased a whole chain of lakes in northern Maine. There were some half-dozen buildings of substantial structure, each being a small bungalow. From the clubroom a green lawn, bedecked with flowers, sloped down to the water, and the pine woods came down to the rear of the camp. The polished hardwood floor was covered with costly rugs.

There were comfortable lounges and spacious, overstuffed armchairs. The clubhouse, like the bungalows, was lit by electric light. The brick fireplace threw out a pleasant warmth in the cool of the autumn evening.

Alonzo Evershay Hollis was one of the leading spirits and richest members of the club. He was only a year or two younger than the elderly judge, and was the president of a large manufacturing corporation. In private life he was benign, suave, and, to all appearance, less merciless than his enemies called him. He had married a second time, late in life — a woman many years his junior. Perhaps it was her influence that had softened him. Certainly they were devoted to each other, and it was agreed that Mrs. Hollis had a more potent influence over him than any of his business associates.

Two other men were in the room. One, Chester Winscombe, was a little over thirty, and one of Hollis' departmental heads, whom the manufacturer had summoned to the club for the purpose of a consultation.

Edwin Carberry, the other, had only arrived an hour or two before, and was to leave the next evening. He was a middle-aged New England man, the head of a concern which had recently been absorbed by Hollis. The manufacturer had invited him to run over from Bangor, where he had business, in order to discuss certain matters.

Hollis pondered. 'If you are correct, civilization hasn't accomplished much,' he said to Judge Segrue.

'Civilization,' Segrue answered, 'is the product of men of normal mentality. But some men and women were born outlaws. Ishmaels, their hands are instinctively against their fellows. One encounters them in every rank of life. Most of them become the victims of their environment. Sometimes, however, a man or woman of this type creates a false adjustment, and becomes an agent of harm to the community. Law cannot contain them. They can neither do justice nor receive it. They should be outlawed.'

'Do you know many such people?' asked Carberry.

'I can name half a dozen prominent and wealthy ones,' answered Segrue.

'You are advocating private justice seriously?' Hollis inquired.

'Quite seriously,' replied Segrue. 'Civilization is not based upon law, but upon an unwritten compact between man and man, between man and woman. It is this latter compact that most of these outlaws violate. When a woman is hanged, or sent to the chair, the law is vindicated — but does not our conscience reproach us?'

Carberry nodded vigorously. 'You're right there, Segrue,' he said with conviction.

'Formerly,' continued Segrue, 'we had a rough and ready instrument of justice in the duel. Its abolition was a mistake.

'Some men are not fit to live.' He turned suddenly to Hollis. 'I am thinking of the Brayton case of many years ago,' he said.

Hollis rocked back in his seat, a brow arched inquisitively, while Carberry remained facially impassive. Not a man answered him. The Judge continued:

'I am speaking among friends. If I am violating the proprieties, as your guest, Hollis, it is because I have always felt deeply upon the subject, although I played no part in the trial. I am convinced that Mrs. Brayton suffered an injustice.'

He glanced at Hollis again for a moment, and went on:

'Brayton, you remember, was a young clerk in Rodman's employment, and happily married. He was sent out of town on a mission. During his absence Mrs. Brayton shot Rodman in his apartment. She claimed that he had persecuted her, had threatened to discharge her husband; that she had gone to him to plead with him, and had shot him in self-defense. She admitted, however, that she had gone there with a revolver, prepared to shoot Rodman unless he promised to retain her husband in his employment and to cease persecuting her.

'Rodman's story was that he had grown tired of her, and that she had shot him deliberately, and of design. In evidence of this he produced certain letters of hers in court. Mrs. Brayton was convicted of an attempt to murder and sent to the penitentiary for five years.'

Segrue glanced at his host again.

'Those letters were *forged*,' he said.

'How could it be proved?' asked Carberry, after a few moments.

'The forger made a verbal confession on his death bed to a hospital attendant. The man repeated it to a friend of mine, a young newspaper man who had always believed in Mrs. Brayton's innocence, and had followed up the case. Subsequently he denied it — bought, no doubt, by the person who was chiefly interested in suppressing the truth. My friend could do nothing; he had no evidence.'

'What happened to the husband?' asked Hollis.

'He divorced his wife and disappeared. He should have stood by her, *believed* her, and — well,' he ended grimly, 'there's my principle of private justice, though, as a judge, I should, of course, carry out my duties under the law.'

''Almost thou persuadest me' — ' quoted Carberry, after a few moments of silence.

Heavy steps sounded outside; the door opened, and a fifth man entered. He looked about fifty years of age. The heavy-featured face was expressive of intense power and unscrupulous resolve. A heavy black mustache partly concealed the flabby jowl.

The eyes were close-set and cunning.

At his entrance a sense of constraint made itself manifest immediately. Segrue's keen blue eyes fixed themselves for a moment upon the face of Chester Winscombe. The young man was staring at the newcomer with a set, bitter look. In another moment the other's glance would have been drawn by it.

Segrue made a sudden sound with his knuckles against the arm of the chair, as if to warn him.

'Hello, Rodman! Had any *luck*?' asked Hollis.

Rodman's face twisted malevolently at Hollis's address. 'Not a thing,' he answered. 'Either there are no fish in Second Lake, or that guide Pierre's a fool, or both. Where are the ladies?'

'Gone for a walk, I believe,' answered Hollis, with a little, involuntary shrug of his shoulders.

But as they spoke feminine voices were heard outside, and a moment later two women entered the room. Mary Rodman was a brunette of attractive and vivacious appearance, about thirty years of age.

Queenie Hollis was a blonde, a few years her senior. Mary Rodman alone would have struck the observer as a remarkably handsome woman, but in the presence of her companion she was almost eclipsed.

Tall, high-colored, with great masses of fair hair piled about her head, Queenie Hollis had also a certain quality of power, in addition to her poise and appearance. One hardly perceived her beauty in that atmosphere of womanly strength. She went to her husband's side and stood there, looking down on him affectionately

'My dear, let me present Mr. Carberry,' said Hollis.

Carberry advanced and bowed; their eyes met in momentary appraisal. At that moment Mary Rodman asked her husband:

'What luck, Eustace?'

'Oh, damn these fool questions! I've answered that one!' Rodman snarled.

In the ensuing moment Segrue touched Chester Winscombe on the arm. Winscombe's eyes were blazing.

'I can't stand this,' the young man muttered.

'Keep quiet!' whispered Segrue.

Mary Rodman, standing with flushed cheeks in the middle of the room, looked utterly humiliated. Queenie Hollis left her husband's side and slipped an arm through hers. It seemed to the Judge as if the two women were protecting each other, in a sort of tacit alliance among women, as if some strong, secret bond united them. But he thought the look on Queenie Hollis's face was more than pity — terror, despair, as if her friend's humiliation was her own.

Chester Winscombe's own eyes never left Mary Rodman's face. As if aware of his scrutiny, Mary turned and gave him a momentary glance of supreme pathos. Rodman and Carberry had left the room. The two men remaining knew the commonplace story. Winscombe and Mary had been engaged three years before. They had had a foolish quarrel, Rodman had come into the girl's life, with his vitality and a certain fascination which he could display in intervals of moroseness, and she had married him in pique. If she had not been bent on thwarting her own happiness she would have discerned his innate crookedness, which made men unwilling to associate with him.

It would have kept him from membership in the fishing club, had Rodman been proposed in the ordinary way, but he had bought the share held by a retiring member, and so evaded the black balls. Everyone, including Pierre, the guide, and Alphonse, the cook, disliked Rodman. Winscombe and he had never met until the day before, and, until his arrival, Winscombe had not seen Mary since their quarrel.

Queenie Hollis broke the silence. 'I'm going to bed,' she said. 'This air's enough to make one want to sleep twelve hours.'

'I second that proposal,' said the Judge.

They said good night to one another, and drifted toward their rooms. With eyes that observed everything, Judge Segrue watched Winscombe go toward his quarters in one of the nearby bungalows. He saw Rodman waiting outside the door, waiting to catch Hollis. The two men met beneath the hall lamp, their faces set like flints, and Segrue, who had been Hollis's lawyer, and was still consulted by him unofficially in his affairs, knew that in the relentless battle which had been set there was to be no quarter.

He knew that the long, private warfare between the two men had reached the breaking point, and that one of the two must inevitably go under.

'Won't you come over to my quarters for a few minutes and smoke a cigar, Hollis?' Segrue heard Rodman ask.

The tones were almost friendly, and yet there sounded something threatening, almost sinister, under the smooth accentuation.

'Not tonight, Rodman,' Hollis answered curtly. 'We would disturb your wife.'

'Oh, my wife's used to being *disturbed*,' said Rodman, with a sneering laugh.

'I'll talk to you tomorrow,' answered Hollis with finality. 'Good night!'

'Better make it tonight,' retorted Rodman. 'There's something of importance that I may want to speak to you about — if you still decline a satisfactory arrangement — something that we haven't taken up yet,' he continued.

There was no mistaking the overt

threat in Rodman's tones now. Rodman swung on his heel and turned away without a word.

Hollis looked after him malevolently. Then his expression changed, and Judge Segrue saw that the evil look on his face embodied, not humiliation, but triumph.

'Going to bed, Segrue?' asked Hollis in the doorway. 'Bit too late to talk, isn't it! But this is my night, in a way. Unless evidences err, *I've* got Eustace Rodman by the throat at last. It's been a long chase, but I've had my hooks into him for a goodish while on account of various things we know about him. It's nip and tuck, but if I win on the showdown I'm going to strip him clean and turn him out into the cold world.'

He laughed at the thought of it, but it was not an evil laugh like Rodman's — only merciless.

'Yes,' he said reflectively, 'I think Rodman's time has come at last. Mind you, Segrue, I'm not holding up that Brayton case against him. That's ancient history. In my opinion a woman who goes to a man's rooms doesn't deserve much sympathy and I guess there wasn't much to choose between them, if the truth were known. I've no use for that kind. She got what she deserved, in my opinion. He got his, too, but it didn't stop him, and he's going to get the rest tomorrow, unless he's got a stronger hand than I imagine he has. The man's a human skunk!'

The two men turned at a rustle, to see Queenie Hollis standing in the hall.

'Are you coming, dear?' she asked.

'By George, yes!' answered her husband. 'We'll fish First Lake together in the morning, Segrue,' he said, 'and then I'll talk about my plans. I've ordered Pierre to call you half an hour before sunrise.'

2

The clubhouse occupied, roughly, the central position in the group of bungalows. It contained, besides the clubroom, the dining room and kitchen, and a two-room suite on the other side of the hall. There were two bedrooms on the upper story. Hollis and his wife occupied the suite below, and Judge Segrue had the large room above them.

On the left of the clubhouse were three bungalows. The nearest was empty, the second was occupied by Carberry, the third by the two servants, Pierre and Alphonse. There were three bungalows to the right, the first being occupied by Chester Winscombe, the second empty, and the outermost by the Rodmans. All the bungalows were well separated from one another, and there were pine trees scattered about the intervening spaces.

In spite of the mountain air, Segrue found sleep impossible that night. After

143

tossing about upon his bed in vain for nearly an hour, he got up, put on his dressing gown, and sat before the window of the living room, looking out upon the moonlit lake. It was partly the remembrance of the remarks he had made in the clubroom that was keeping him awake. Never before had he expressed his secret opinions with such frankness.

He had surprised himself, but it had seemed to him that the advancement of his theory had been singularly appropriate. For, if ever a man could be described as human scum, that man was Rodman.

He was the crookedest man spiritually whom he had ever known. He had broken the unwritten compact with almost all men, and all women. The old Judge thought of Mary Rodman, with her hopeless love for Chester Winscombe, writhing under the lash of the bully's tongue. It was a miserable chance that had thrown Winscombe and Mary Rodman together in such surroundings. Neither of them had imagined the possibility of such a meeting, and Segrue had seen that night that it would take very little on Rodman's part to precipitate an outburst on the part of the younger man.

If only some man whom he had wronged had taken Rodman by the throat and strangled him years before; what a sum of misery would have been avoided!

The Judge was about to go back to his bed at last when he began to be aware of the sound of voices beneath him. Mrs. Hollis was apparently making some earnest request of her husband, but his answers were indistinguishable.

Involuntarily Segrue found himself listening to her excited tones. They appeared almost abandoned in their entreaty; yet recklessness and undisciplined emotion were the last qualities which the Judge would have associated with Queenie Hollis.

'I'm asking this for Mary's sake, Lonnie,' he heard her plead. 'I heard what you were saying to Judge Segrue before we went to bed, and I can't sleep for thinking of it. You know what Mary's life has been with that man; you can picture to yourself what it would be with him when they are devoid of even the ordinary comforts of existence.'

Now Segrue was able to distinguish Hollis's answer.

'Don't trouble about that, my dear,' he said. 'Rodman will fall upon his feet. I can't exactly imagine him begging on the streets, or doing manual labor. Besides, it isn't likely that they'll stay together long. Three years of that sort of life is most women's limit.'

'Lonnie, you don't understand Mary!' cried his wife. 'She's not that kind. She'd never leave him in poverty. She'd stick to him as long as he needed her. That's her kind.'

'Well, you bet Rodman won't stick to her — in poverty, anyway,' her husband answered. 'And it'll prove the best thing that could happen to her. You know how much a divorce would mean to her and Winscombe.'

'Mary doesn't believe in divorce.'

'They'll all say that. She will someday,' answered Hollis grimly. 'I wouldn't have sent for Winscombe if I'd thought that there would be any chance of their meeting here. I didn't imagine Rodman was coming up here to beg off what's coming

146

to him. But now that they have met, I'm going to keep Winscombe here as long as Rodman stays, and see that they have a chance to talk things over. You know, Queenie, I *never* understood why you and Mary are *so* devoted, and I've hated it because it's forced me to be civil to Rodman. And it seems to me you're mighty anxious about him.'

'Oh, *it's for her!*' cried Queenie, in anguish. 'That's why it's all wrong, what you're proposing to do. Take what's yours, but don't strip them! Leave them enough to live in comfort!'

'Oh, I guess he'll make enough to keep the wolf from the door,' Hollis's deep rumble answered. 'You speak as if I wanted them to starve. But I mean to strip that vermin to his hide, and throw him out of the sort of decent society he's got into.

'Judge Segrue was talking in the club-room tonight,' he continued. 'He said such men as Rodman aren't fit to live, and someone ought to take them by the throat and kill them. I agreed with him. I can't kill Rodman physically, but I'm going to put him out socially and financially.

'No, you're wrong, dear. You know I

wouldn't refuse you a single thing in reason. But I just can't see it your way. As I look at it, it will mean a merciful release for Mary, either by his act or by hers. If I didn't know you, Queenie, I'd almost think that it was pity for Rodman made you ask me to spare him.'

'Pity for him? For him, after the way you saw him treat his wife tonight? It's for her, Lonnie! Do it for me, then! Do it for my sake!'

Again Hollis's tones became inaudible; but presently Segrue, in his room above, could hear Queenie Hollis's hysterical sobbing underneath.

He sat uncomfortable by the window, hating himself for having overheard the altercation. Then once more Hollis's voice burst out, in furious tones:

'For two pins I'd put a bullet through the skunk, Queenie! He's brought nothing but harm to everyone he's ever come in contact with. And now he's upset you! That's the last straw!'

The last straw was the last of the dialogue that was audible. For twenty minutes longer Judge Segrue sat there, looking out at the lake. He was just beginning to recover his equanimity, and to think of going back to bed, when his attention was suddenly attracted by a figure moving in front of the bungalows.

It was the figure of a man, but the moon was low behind a bank of clouds, and it was impossible to distinguish more than the faint outlines. Segrue watched it move stealthily toward the end bungalow at the right — Rodman's.

The bungalows were not in alignment, and from his window the Judge could see the rear, as well as the front, of each. Now, of a sudden, he perceived a second, a woman's figure, standing at Rodman's back door.

The first figure did not seem aware of her proximity. It vanished from view behind a clump of pines. Judge Segrue drew his head back quickly. He had done enough eavesdropping that night; he did not mean to play the spy as well. But his heart misgave him. Who could these nocturnal prowlers be but Chester Winscombe and Mary Rodman, engaged in a clandestine meeting?

He had not thought such a thing possible of either. There had seemed something brave and heroic about each of them, about the way they had met, after those years of suffering and embitterment, with a simple hand clasp. And yet he could not find it in his heart altogether to blame them. He knew what their love had been.

But what cross-purposes were at work among that little group of men and women who had met by accident at the fishing club! And the black heart of the storm was Rodman! Only by his death could the fellow make requital for the wrongs that he had done — his breaches of the unwritten human compact.

Shaking his head, the Judge went back to bed. But still he could not sleep. He was contrasting Rodman with Hollis, Mary Rodman with Queenie. At last he dozed off without realizing it, and had just fallen asleep when two sharp sounds brought him back suddenly to consciousness.

They seemed to roar through his brain, as if the whole universe had fallen, and yet he realized they had been too faint in reality to have awakened him unless he had been subconsciously expecting them. And he knew now that he had. Every nerve had been tense in him that night, in expectation of something of that kind, although he had not at the time been aware of it.

It had been the double discharge of a firearm.

The Judge sat up, listening. Surely no dream could have produced that stunning auditory effect, although he began to be aware that he had been moving in a dim nightmare of phantasmal figures, a menacing crowd, with hands outstretched toward a central form — Rodman.

And still the echoes of the two shots seemed to ring in his ears, and into his mind there stole slowly the awful consciousness of murder.

It was a sixth sense acquired through years of professional work. The Judge had always known unerringly a man whose hands were stained with blood, since he had ascended the bench. It seemed an eternity before anything began to happen. Then the Judge heard steps upon the porch of the clubhouse; Hollis began coming up the stairs.

Segrue was out of bed and in his dressing gown by the time Hollis's sounded. He opened the door.

'This is awful, Segrue!' Hollis said in a harsh whisper. 'Rodman has been shot dead!'

'Just a minute, Hollis, and I'll be with you,' the Judge answered.

Without putting on his socks, he thrust his bare feet into his boots, and quickly fastened the laces. He put on his coat and trousers and accompanied his host down the stairs.

Pierre and Alphonse were standing at the open door of the clubhouse. As they reached the hall Queenie Hollis opened the door of the apartment and stood before them, a wrap about her, and her hair streaming about her shoulders.

'What is it? What's the matter?' she asked, turning a frightened gaze upon them.

Her face was ghastly white in the faint moonlight.

'I — I've been so sound asleep. Where have you been, Lonnie? I didn't hear you go out.'

'It's — an accident, dear,' answered her husband. 'Go back to bed. Judge Segrue and I are going to see about it.'

'Is it — is it Mr. Rodman?' she gasped. 'I thought I heard a shot from the end bungalow. He's — he's dead?'

'I don't know. I went out when I heard it and met these men. I hoped you wouldn't wake.' He patted her shoulder. 'Go back to bed, Queenie,' he said, 'and try not to let yourself be overcome.'

She went back inside the room obediently, and closed the door. Pierre explained excitedly as they hurried toward Rodman's bungalow:

'We heard somebody moving about the camp, Alphonse and me,' he pattered. 'We sleep ver' light since the thieves stole the boat last month. Alphonse and me went down to the lake, but the boats were all right. Just then we hear the two shots — *bang, bang!* They come from Monsieur Rodman's bungalow. We run there and look t'rough the window. Just then I see Mrs. Rodman turn out the light in the bedroom. Monsieur Rodman is lying dead in the living room, and Monsieur

Winscombe stands beside him.'

'My God!' muttered Hollis. He seized Pierre by the arm. 'Did he have a revolver?' he demanded

'No, no, Monsieur, I don't see dat,' Pierre replied

Hollis turned to Segrue. 'That proves nothing,' he cried. 'You couldn't hang a dog on that!'

Segrue did not reply. They had reached the bungalow. The door was open, the lamp still alight in the living room. Rodman was lying on the floor, stone dead, with blood on his breast. Mary Rodman crouched in a chair beside the body, her face in her hands.

Chester Winscombe was still standing beside the dead man. But his expression showed that he was perfectly resolute and self-possessed, and his attitude was almost that of a lounger.

3

After saying good night in the clubroom,
Chester Winscombe had gone to his
bungalow next to the clubhouse and flung
himself into a chair. He sat there for a
long time, fighting such devils of temptation as he had never imagined could
possibly assail anyone.

They seemed to fill the room — living,
though formless, entities, crowding about
him, shouting out their taunts and
commands. And the burden of these was:
'Kill him! Kill him now, to win the
woman you love and take her away!'

He had known, during the brief instant
that Mary Rodman's glance met his the
day before, when they came face to face
with each other, that she *still* loved him.
The years had slipped away and they were
back in memory in the old days, when
they meant everything to each other, and
had their lives before them.

Mary's marriage with Rodman had

horrified Winscombe. He had put her out of his mind and tried to mask his love with contempt that she should have sold herself for money. But in the instant of their meeting he had known that was not true; he had understood everything, and had forgiven her. Nothing had mattered since, except that they loved each other.

When Rodman had abused her in the presence of the company, Winscombe had only been restrained by Judge Segrue from hurling himself upon his enemy. Segrue's words in the clubroom had burned like coals into his heart. Death was the only destiny for such a cur as Rodman.

Now, sitting alone in his room, he felt the temptation an overwhelming one. He did not weigh his chances of escape. He thought only of Mary, doomed to a life of shame and humiliation with the brute she had married.

He could no longer resist. He went to his kit-bag and took out an automatic pistol with which he had been used to practice at the Pistol Club; he had brought it with him with a view to engaging in target practice at the camp, to keep his hand in. Automatically, and hardly conscious of what he was doing, he loaded the magazine, and put the weapon in his pocket.

He hesitated at the door. In the back of his mind was still the resolution not to kill Rodman, but all his mental powers seemed numbed in the presence of the overwhelming desire to free Mary from the brute to whom she was bound. Yet vaguely there was shaping in his mind some compromise. He knew Rodman stayed up late going through his papers. If he confronted him, Rodman *might* fire first, or in some way give him his justification.

It was all very vaguely outlined, and, in fact, impossible, but Winscombe hesitated only a moment before stepping out softly into the half-dark of the moon.

No lights showed in the clubhouse, but, as he had expected, there was the glimmer of one behind the shades of Rodman's living room. The rear room, in which the Rodmans slept, was dark.

Suddenly, as Winscombe neared the

bungalow, he saw the shadow of Rodman thrown at full length on the shade. An instant later it was joined by another shadow — that of a woman.

Winscombe stepped back into the group of pine trees nearby. His brain was working very clearly now, and he was ice cold with resolution. Of course he would not eavesdrop; but, when Mary Rodman had gone back to her room, he knew that nothing on earth could keep him from shooting Rodman, for she was pleading with him. He could not hear a sound from the place where he lurked, but there was a strange, pathetic shadow-play of the figures upon the shade. Winscombe saw Mary's arms raised in entreaty, saw Rodman shake his head and make a gesture of his hand in negation: it was a pantomime in silhouette that Winscombe watched in fascination and horror.

But when he saw Mary fall on her knees with hands clasped in agonized appeal, the last vestige of his irresolution left him. The sight of the woman he loved kneeling to her husband resolved him to shoot the brute down in his tracks like a dog, without parley or ceremony.

And he stepped out from the shelter of the pines. A few steps brought him to the door of the bungalow. Now he could hear the girl's low voice, pleading wildly, and Rodman's sneering tones, although the words that either spoke were indistinguishable.

Then Rodman's shadow appeared alone, indistinct and blurring, as the man moved round the lamp on the table.

Though the shade was down, the window was wide open, and between the edge of the shade and the window frame Winscombe could see a slice of the room, and the edge of an open, unshaded window on the opposite side. Leaning sidewise from the rustic porch, Winscombe placed his fingertips upon the shade, and drew it imperceptibly outward.

The instant Rodman's figure filled that slice of space he meant to fire. Still holding the edge of the shade with his left hand, Winscombe inserted the tip of the muzzle of the automatic between the shade and the window frame, waiting for Rodman to come into view.

Suddenly he heard Rodman utter a sharp exclamation. He thought himself discovered. There followed a tussle in the room, a woman's cry. Rodman was swaying in grotesque silhouette upon the shade. Two shots rang out. Rodman's cry answered hers, but in a strangled splutter. Momentarily blinded by the twin flashes of Rodman's shots, Hollis blinkingly saw him staggering, spinning, one hand clutching his breast, the other a revolver. Smoke drifted through the aperture of the window. There followed the thud of Rodman's fall.

And Winscombe had not fired!

Instantly Winscombe sprang forward and pulled at the door handle. The door swung open. He entered. The bedroom door was closing. As he entered, there sounded the snap of an electric light button.

The interior of the bedroom became invisible before the door had closed. Yet the last half-second of illumination disclosed the glimpse of a woman's white garment disappearing within the room. The door slammed, the key clicked in the lock upon the other side. Silence ensued.

Winscombe laid his automatic down upon the table and tried to think. He must act with an ordered judgment, but in the shock of the situation all his instincts were to perform mechanical actions instead. He pulled himself together and bent over Rodman.

The man was lying twisted up upon the floor, and Winscombe saw that he had died practically instantaneously. Only a trickle of blood came from the breast, but the pallor of death was already creeping over the face, which had begun to assume an inhuman aspect, as if the evil forces in Rodman's soul were already taking possession of his mortal remnants.

Rodman's hand still clutched the revolver with which he had fired back at his assassin, and the fingers, contracting in the death struggle, were flattened against the handle.

Winscombe turned away and looked at the table. He knew that Rodman had brought a number of papers with him, in order to go through them with Hollis on the morrow, in his endeavor to escape Hollis's punishment. He seemed to have been arranging them, for they lay scattered about upon the table.

There were also letters, tied and piled up neatly in a little case by the electric lamp.

After a moment's hesitation, Winscombe went to the locked door communicating with the bedroom, and tapped on it. There was no response, but there came the sound of hurrying footsteps on the other side. Winscombe tapped again, more loudly. Then he put his lips to the crevice of the door.

'Mary! Please come out at once! I must speak to you! Don't be afraid of me!' he called to the woman behind.

The sound of footsteps ceased. A soft rustling followed. Winscombe repeated his appeal more urgently. He had the intimate sense of Mary Rodman on the other side of the door, her face barely an inch or two from his. That door was like the intangible but iron law that had kept them apart so long. He heard her hurried breathing. And suddenly the key clicked in the lock again, and Mary Rodman stood in the entrance. She was fully dressed, and she looked at him with haggard eyes.

'*You*, Winscombe!' she whispered, with indrawn, agitated breath.

She burst into hysterical laughter, and put her hands over her face, and still she laughed and laughed. Winscombe drew them forcibly away, and held them.

'Listen to me, Mary!' he cried. 'I want to *save you*. I'm speaking now as I used to speak to you years ago, and you know we never lied to each other. I came here tonight under a mad impulse to shoot him down in his tracks, like a dog, because he had no right to live after his brutal insult to you last evening. I should probably have killed him if *you* hadn't. Because that thought was in my mind, I'm going to take the guilt upon myself.'

She stared at him incredulously.

'Upon yourself!' she whispered.

'Because I *meant* to shoot him, and because you did right, Mary. Judge Segrue was saying last night that he should have been killed long ago. Perhaps that influenced me. Anyway, *I* shot him. Remember that: *I shot him!*'

163

Suddenly the girl dropped into a chair, covered her face with her hands again, and abandoned herself to a wild outburst of grief. Winscombe glanced at the dead man, and back at her.

'Mary, you *must* let me save you,' he said. 'Quick! Where's the revolver that you killed him with?'

But she paid not the least attention to him, only sat still in the chair, except for the convulsive shudders that ran through her body. Winscombe pleaded with her in vain; she appeared utterly deaf to his words, and overcome with fear. The sound of voices outside the bungalow reached Winscombe's ears. He shook the girl by the shoulders.

'Mary, for God's sake pull yourself together!' he whispered. 'They're coming! Remember, I did it! It's for your sake! Where's the weapon you used? Quick!'

She looked at him for an instant, her eyes like a doomed soul's.

'Chester — *go!*' she sobbed.

Winscombe's mind acted with the speed of lightning. He straightened himself and waited till the newcomers were at the door; then, snatching up his automatic, which he had laid down on the table, he swept back his arm and hurled it through the open window at the side of the bungalow into the lake. He turned to see Hollis and Judge Segrue, with the frightened faces of the guides behind. He thrust out his arm dramatically and pointed at Rodman's body.

'*I* killed him! You *know* why I did it!' he raved; and, plunging past them, he rushed into the darkness.

He ran down to the lake-edge, entered a canoe, took up the paddle and pushed out from the shore. The two men, watching him in stupefaction, saw his figure come into view a minute or two later, paddling violently across a stretch of moonlit water. Then it vanished among the shadows of the trees.

4

Judge Segrue stooped over the body of Rodman, peering into the face.

'Dead — stone dead!' he said briefly.

He stood up and looked at Hollis, then at Mary in the chair. The girl sat just as she had done at the moment of their entrance; she had neither uncovered her face nor stirred.

'Mrs. Rodman, you must let my wife take care of you,' said Hollis, huskily. 'This has been a dreadful shock to you. Come with me!'

Mary Rodman rose with an effort. At that moment Queenie Hollis appeared at the entrance.

'I couldn't stay *there*, Lonnie,' she whispered. 'I know Mr. Rodman is dead. I've come for Mary.'

She caught sight of the body on the floor, and began trembling violently. Hollis put his arm about her in support.

'Who did it?' she whispered.

Nobody answered her. The two men were watching Mary Rodman. Something in the rigidity of her poise made them momentarily regardless of Queenie Hollis. Then she pointed at the floor.

'What's *that*?' she cried. 'Whose is it?'

The Judge and Hollis became aware of a trail of blood spots on the floor. They began some distance from the body, and ran to the porch, splattering the steps of the bungalow.

Judge Segrue sprang to Mary's side. The girl was falling. With a sigh she collapsed into his arms in absolute unconsciousness.

'Let's get her to your rooms, Hollis,' said the Judge.

They carried her to the clubhouse, Queenie Hollis following. They placed her on the sofa in the living room and left her, Queenie kneeling at her side, applying restoratives. When they got back to the bungalow the servants were still waiting.

'Hollis, may I give orders?' asked the Judge. 'Pierre, you keep guard and let no one enter. Alphonse, you'll relieve Pierre at sunrise. And you saw Winscombe throw the pistol into the lake. Go down and see if you can find it. It ought to be in the shallows under the bank.'

Hollis and he tried to follow the trail of bloodspots outside the door, but lost them a few paces away.

'It looks as if Rodman's bullet grazed Winscombe,' said the Judge. 'Well, nothing more can be done till daylight. I'd advise you to move into the room opposite mine, and try to get some sleep.'

He caught Hollis by the arm as he was about to re-enter the bungalow.

'I wouldn't go back there,' he said, 'especially in the darkness. There may be *other* footprints — it's always best to make as few journeys as possible.'

Hollis, who seemed dazed by the developments, assented, and retraced his steps.

'And now,' continued Segrue, 'I shall have to call up the authorities.'

'That means Winscombe's capture,' muttered Hollis.

'I think he's the sort of man who'll return when he's thought matters over. He behaved more foolishly than he realized at the time,' said Segrue.

'You mean — you think he — good

heavens, Segrue, you don't mean he's shielding — ?'

Judge Segrue closed his lips tightly.

'Hollis, you know I'm not prepared to answer that,' he replied, greatly moved. 'We have the same evidence, the same ability to form conclusions — at least — '

He broke off. They went back to the clubhouse in silence. Going to the telephone, the Judge called up the sheriff in Mayville, a small town a few miles away. When he got the connection, he gave a brief outline of the events of the night in the baldest manner, omitting no essential detail. In reply he was told that the sheriff and a county detective would start at once with a buckboard, to take in the body.

When he had finished telephoning, to Hollis's surprise he next phoned for a large New England city. Having got long distance and given the number, Judge Segrue hung up the receiver, and, during the wait of twenty minutes that ensued, he paced the hall without speaking. Hollis, seated on the stairs, watched him wearily; he seemed broken by the tragedy. The telephone rang at last, and Judge

Segrue gave a name unknown to Hollis, asking that a Mr. Pettibone come to the camp immediately. He gave careful instructions as to the route, hung up the receiver, and came back.

'That was a friend of mine,' he explained. 'I want him here for reasons of my own. You've no objections, Hollis?'

'Not the least in the world,' replied Hollis, with weary indifference.

'And now,' Segrue continued, 'if I were you, I'd follow my own example and try to get to sleep. The worst part's coming in a few hours' time, and the sheriff and the detective ought to reach the camp by daylight. I envy Carberry, sleeping through it all,' he added, glancing up at the silent bungalow on the left of the clubhouse.

Hollis and Segrue withdrew to their bedrooms. Neither of the men slept, however. Judge Segrue closed his eyes and lay down in his clothes; but his mind kept following the details of the tragedy. He shook his head and frowned; he hated being mixed up in the business.

Judge Segrue rose at dawn and found Hollis huddling in the clubroom. A little after sunrise the sheriff and the detective drove into the camp. The sheriff was a typical small-town official of about fifty, alert and practical. County Detective Askew, the name by which he introduced his companion, was a younger man, keen and wide awake; he carried a large bag with him.

A few minutes after the arrival of the buckboard, while the four men were still grouped in front of the clubhouse, Carberry emerged from his bungalow.

He was armed with a fishing rod and gaff, and received the news of the events with manifest dismay.

'I wanted to leave for Bangor this evening,' he said to Hollis. 'I suppose it will be impossible for us to talk things over under the circumstances.'

'You can't wait over a day or two?'

'I might,' reflected Carberry. 'Let me see — '

'I'd be very sorry to miss our opportunity of getting together,' said Hollis, 'but I'm hardly able to do justice to my end today, as you'll realize. Stay over the weekend!'

'Well — I will!' Carberry answered.

The sheriff and Detective Askew listened to Hollis and the Judge as they gave their versions of what had occurred. Pierre, under examination, repeated the story that he had already told.

'It's too bad,' said the sheriff. 'Young Winscombe hasn't a chance. We've telephoned all the district, and he'll be arrested wherever he comes out of the woods. Trouble is, some fool may shoot at him. I guess he'll come back here, though, when he begins to realize his position.'

He turned to Pierre.

'You say you saw Mrs. Rodman turn out the light after the shots were fired?' he inquired.

'Yes, Monsieur, I swear it.'

The sheriff and the detective exchanged glances. Hollis interpreted them in the obvious way.

'Any trouble between her and her husband?' drawled Askew.

Hollis hesitated.

'Well — you know what married people are,' he answered. 'They may not have been in complete agreement, but I tell you Mary Rodman is absolutely incapable — '

Judge Segrue nudged him and whispered a few words in his ear. Hollis shook his head, then nodded.

'Judge Segrue thinks it advisable for me to add *every* material fact,' he continued, with manifest reluctance. 'I may as well tell you, then, that Mr. Winscombe and Mrs. Rodman were once engaged to be married. If I hesitated to mention this, it is simply because I am disinclined to speak about private matters.'

Neither of the two newcomers spoke for a moment or two. Then the sheriff turned to his companion.

'Well, we may as well take a look at the bungalow,' he suggested.

They went inside and at once proceeded to make their examination of the dead man.

'Mighty powerful *pistol*,' commented the detective. 'Ball passed clean through the body. It was nickel pointed, I would say. One of the newest types of automatic. High velocity, too — you see, the wound's no bigger at the back than in the front. I'd call it difficult to say for sure whether he was shot from the front or the back, wouldn't you, Mr. Bowles?'

He broke the revolver in the dead man's hand and spun the chamber round. One shot had been fired.

'Found any traces of a ball in here?' he asked.

'We've made no examination,' answered Hollis.

They hunted without result. The sheriff gave his opinion that the bullet which killed Rodman had been fired from the door and had passed out of the opposite window. It was impossible to say how Rodman had been standing; he had fallen in a twisted heap.

They examined the trail of blood spots, and lost them a few paces from the door. There were no signs of more, either about the bungalow or at the little pier from which Winscombe had taken the canoe.

'Looks as if Rodman grazed him,' the sheriff commented, 'but not enough to do much damage. Mighty quick on the draw he must have been, to have winged him in the darkness. Well, I guess my part of this job's ended. I'll take in the body for the inquest, and then I'll have to superintend the hunt for Mr. Winscombe, though I guess he'll surrender himself here today, if he's got sense. Mr. Askew will remain here and handle the case, and bring him in if he turns up. Not much of a mystery, I guess.'

After a pick-up breakfast, the body was wrapped in blankets and placed on the vehicle. There came a colloquy between the sheriff and Detective Askew, at the end of which the former went up to Hollis.

'Mr. Askew suggests swearing in your two men as deputies,' he said. 'I guess that might be the best thing, seeing that you and the Judge are friends of young Winscombe's. It'll give them legal powers covering his arrest.'

He did not refer to the right to shoot, but the others understood.

Alphonse and Pierre were accordingly sworn in, and their duties explained to them.

'You two gentlemen will, of course, remain at the camp until the inquest,' said the sheriff. 'No need to say that.'

'Will you want me?' asked Carberry.

'I guess not, but anyway you'll be staying over, I think I heard you say. I'll notify you by telephone, Mr. Hollis,' he added.

'I'd like to see the ladies as soon as possible,' said Askew, when the vehicle had driven away. 'And I'd be particularly glad of your help, Judge, in examining them,' he added.

'You'll have to excuse me,' answered Judge Segrue. 'I've given you the facts so far as I know them. I'm a material witness, and stand prepared to render you any service that you are legally entitled to demand of me. But I must absolutely decline to go beyond that point.'

He spoke with emotion, and Hollis thought he had aged ten years since the evening before. Detective Askew glanced thoughtfully at him; then looked at Hollis.

'Just as you say, of course, Judge,' he answered quietly. 'I guess you know your rights.'

'I should prefer the ladies not to be disturbed for another hour at least,' said Hollis. 'That is, unless you consider it absolutely necessary, Mr. Askew. They have had a hard night of it, and you'll realize this has been a great shock to Mrs. Rodman. Do you intend to arrest her?'

'Oh, I guess there'll be no hurry about that,' answered Askew, easily. 'Anyway, I'll wait a while before seeing them. I'd like you to come back to the Rodman bungalow with me. I suppose no one has been inside since the murder, has there?'

'No, the men have been on guard,' replied Hollis.

'I'd like that to remain for the present,' said the detective, as they entered the bungalow. 'There's a lot of papers here,' he continued, pointing to the littered table. 'Business matters, I suppose. How long had Mr. Rodman come in for?'

'Only a few days, I believe,' Hollis answered.

'Been here long?'

'Since Thursday.'

'You don't know anything about these, I suppose?' asked the detective, indicating the papers.

'I believe I do,' answered Hollis. 'In fact, they have reference to me. Mr.

Rodman and I had some affairs to settle. I suppose,' he added, 'they can be sealed for his executors?'

'The court will have to order that. I'll have to take charge of them. I'll put them together later. Most likely I'll be through by sundown. You don't know if Mr. Winscombe had any business troubles with Mr. Rodman?'

'I'm certain he hadn't. Mr. Winscombe is in my own employment. By the way, you'll realize that I don't wish my private transactions with Mr. Rodman to become public property?'

He glanced at the papers. The detective's eyes met Hollis's in a keen, scrutinizing gaze.

'Oh, sure, that'll be all right,' he answered. 'By the way, have you any rifles in the camp?'

'There are a couple of hunting rifles in the rack in the hall,' said Hollis. 'Pierre was cleaning them yesterday.'

'I'd like the deputy to carry one.'

'But — ?' began Hollis.

'Say, what's to prevent young Winscombe returning at night and arming himself? You can never tell. Anyway, I'd like to look at them.'

He accompanied Hollis back to the clubhouse. The Judge, who was standing on the steps, moved quietly away as they approached. Inside the hall two rifles stood side by side in a rack. Detective Askew examined each in turn.

'You say your man cleaned these yesterday?' he asked.

'Yes, I watched him.'

'Where d'you keep your rags and polishing materials? In there? Cupboard not locked, I see. This rifle was cleaned later than the other — in the dark, I'd say.'

'What d'you mean?' demanded Hollis.

'Cleaned by a man in a hurry. Too much oil altogether. The stock's soaked with it.' He broke the breech and squinted down the barrel. 'Take a look,' he said, holding up the weapon by the muzzle toward the light.

'The barrel's not been cleaned!' Hollis exclaimed.

'It's been fouled by a shot,' answered Detective Askew. 'The stock was polished afterward to remove traces of fingerprints.

And the trigger's dripping with oil, put here for the same purpose. *This* is the weapon that was used to kill Mr. Rodman!'

'But — but — ' Hollis stammered.

'Fact,' said Askew briefly. 'I guessed it was a rifle bullet soon as I saw the wound. With your permission,' he continued, 'I'll see the ladies now.'

Hollis, moving as if stupefied by the revelation, tapped at the door of the apartment. Almost immediately his wife opened it. She was fully dressed, her face was flushed, and there were dark rings around her eyes.

'My dear, this is Detective Askew,' announced her husband. 'He wants to ask a few questions of you and Mary.'

'Very well,' answered Mrs. Hollis mechanically, coming out into the hall.

'I'll begin with Mrs. Rodman, if I may,' said Askew.

'Will you ask Mary to step outside?' suggested Hollis to his wife. 'Tell her I don't think the ordeal will be a prolonged one.' He glanced almost appealingly at the detective.

'Why, Mary isn't in *here*! Isn't she with *you*?' exclaimed Mrs. Hollis.

'Mary?' cried her husband. 'I haven't seen her since last night. When did she leave you?'

'I don't know. I've been asleep some time. I was utterly worn out. When I awoke half an hour ago she wasn't here.'

5

'Segrue! Segrue! Come here!' cried Hollis, speaking now in uncontrolled excitement. 'Mary's gone — left the camp an hour or more ago.'

Judge Segrue hurried up, followed by Carberry. 'What's that you say?' he asked. 'When did she leave?' he continued, turning to Mrs. Hollis.

'I don't know anything about it,' replied Queenie Hollis, in the same mechanical manner. 'I stayed beside her for a long time last night. She was only half conscious. I thought toward morning she had fallen asleep, and I let my eyes close, and — that's all I knew till half an hour ago, when I awoke and found she was not in the apartment.'

She turned to her husband. 'Lonnie, she *must* be found! She may be half delirious!' she cried.

'She was in a terrible state when you brought her here last night.'

'Then the first thing to do is to consider which way she's likely to have gone,' said Judge Segrue. 'If she's taken the Mayville road she'll be found and taken care of. Best not to start inquiries over the phone, Hollis. Probably it's the lake trail or a canoe. We'll see if one's missing. Anyway, she's not likely to have gone far.'

The three men hurried down toward the water, leaving Detective Askew with Mrs. Hollis. Askew turned to her.

'I understand you were not a witness of the crime?' he asked.

'No, indeed, thank God!' exclaimed Mrs. Hollis, fervently. 'My husband wouldn't let me leave this apartment.'

'But you went to the Rodman bungalow?'

'I ran out at last. I couldn't bear to be left here alone. I went to the bungalow door, and — and saw Mr. Rodman's body. Mary Rodman fell down in a faint, and I came back here with her.'

'What were the relations between Mrs. Rodman and her husband?'

'Well, they were not very happy together, I believe,' answered Queenie

Hollis reluctantly.

'Any reason to suppose that Mrs. Rodman and Chester Winscombe cared for each other?'

'Oh, they may have done in the past. But it's too awful to suggest that either of them murdered Mr. Rodman. Mary couldn't hurt a fly. It's *impossible*, I tell you, *impossible*!'

'One more question, Mrs. Hollis,' said Askew. 'Your husband was awakened by the shots and went out?'

'Yes — *yes!*'

'Leaving you asleep?'

'He didn't want to wake me, of course. I awoke when I heard him coming back into the clubhouse.'

'You are a sound sleeper?'

'Not particularly, but I didn't hear the shots.'

'Thank you. You say neither Mr. Winscombe nor Mrs. Rodman could have been guilty of the crime. Whom *do* you suspect, then, Mrs. Hollis?'

He turned suddenly and shot the question at her. Queenie Hollis started violently.

'I — I — *nobody!*' she cried. 'It's all *incredible* to me.'

'May I glance inside your apartment for a moment?'

She stepped aside grudgingly, and Askew entered the living room, went to the connecting door, and took in the bedroom with a single glance. When he went out the three men were coming up from the lake.

'She didn't cross the lake,' said Judge Segrue. 'There's only one canoe missing. We're going to take the lake trail, and we'll take a rifle and fire at intervals, in case she's within hearing. I suppose you won't need us for a few hours?'

'Not at all,' answered the detective.

'We'll be back by sundown,' said Hollis, 'if we don't find her, and you'll probably have had word in that case that she's been located on the Mayville road. If Mrs. Rodman hasn't been found we'll call in help and scour the country.'

He went inside and spoke to his wife for a few minutes, coming out with two letters, which he placed in a rack on the hall table. 'My wife's — to the stores, countermanding orders for provisions,' he explained, seeing Askew glance at them. 'If you want to *read them*, you may,' he added, sarcastically, as if a little affronted that Askew had been inside the apartment.

'Not at all, Mr. Hollis,' disclaimed the detective politely.

And he made his way toward the Rodman bungalow. A few minutes later he saw the three men going down the trail, Hollis carrying the rifle. He watched them until they were out of sight, then went inside.

Askew had brought the equipment for a murder case, and at once began moving about the living room and bedroom, making thin deposits of lead oxide in likely places, for the purpose of bringing out fingerprints. The results he photographed with a small enlarging camera, developing the films in a cupboard, which he converted into a suitable darkroom.

He came out and stood surveying the results with a puckered brow. Then he sat down and went over them with a pocket glass. Apparently puzzled, he hung up the films to dry and directed his attention to the papers on Rodman's table.

He could make out little, except that they involved some transactions between Rodman and Hollis.

Then he turned his attention to the letters in the case. At once he became serious. He read several of them through.

They were love letters, addressed to Rodman by some unknown woman, and of an uncompromising — or most compromising — character.

'Queer duck,' he cogitated, 'to carry them about with him, when he'd brought his wife along on the trip! Unless — '

He slipped one of the letters into his pocket and put the remainder back. He went out on the porch. Alphonse, who had relieved Pierre, was seated on the wooden steps, his rifle beside him, munching at a slab of bread and meat. At this moment Pierre came hurrying up, holding something in his hand.

'Behold, Monsieur, I have found it!' exclaimed the guide.

He held out Winscombe's dripping automatic. The detective took the weapon, opened the magazine, and dropped the cartridges into his hand. The chamber had been full; the weapon obviously had not been fired.

'All right,' said Askew. 'Wait a moment. Has anybody been inside this bungalow since the murder?'

'No, Monsieur,' said both the men, promptly.

'Nobody tried to get in?'

'Mr. Hollis wished to enter,' Pierre recollected, 'but Judge Segrue forbade him.'

'When was this?' demanded Askew.

'Just after Monsieur Rodman's body was found, Monsieur.'

'And nobody else?'

'No, Monsieur.' Both men were positive on that point.

'All right,' said the detective, after pondering for a moment. 'There's no need for either of you two men to keep guard any more. I'll attend to it. Take that rifle back to the rack. I shall not need either of you for the present. You understand your duties as deputies?'

Alphonse assented volubly. He had acted as a deputy two years before, in a neighboring county. Askew impressed upon them that they were *bound* to render him any assistance that he might demand of them, and dismissed them.

Satisfied at last, Askew left the bungalow. Queenie Hollis was seated on the steps. At the sight of him she rose pointedly and re-entered her apartment. She did not emerge during the remainder of the morning. At noon Askew tapped at her door and asked if he could have lunch sent in to her, but she declined curtly, speaking through an inch of opened door.

Askew smiled. He had the cook bring him something to eat, and took up his position on the clubhouse steps. During the greater part of the afternoon he was aware of Queenie Hollis's quick glances at him from behind the drawn shades of the living room.

It was evident to the detective that he had offended her, but he hardly thought of that. He was busy weaving the threads of the net which he was drawing about the murderer, and he believed that he had his evidence practically complete. Once or twice he went back to the bungalow to reassure himself; at last he packed the films away, slung his case about him, and awaited the return of the searchers.

From time to time during the course of the day Askew heard the rifle shots of the search party across the lake, but when the three men returned late in the afternoon, Mary Rodman was not with them.

'No news?' inquired the Judge anxiously of the detective.

'Not a word,' answered Askew. 'I just called up Mayville. Nothing seen of her. You found no tracks?'

'Not a sign,' said Hollis anxiously. 'We followed the trail as far as the top of the mountain. We'll have to organize a big search party.'

'Pretty late now,' said Askew, glancing at the setting sun. 'Can't do much in the woods at night.'

Queenie Hollis, hearing the voices, came out of her room. She had overheard the gist of the conversation.

'Lonnie, she *must* be found!' she cried hysterically. 'She can't be left to spend the night alone in the woods.'

Hollis turned to Judge Segrue with an

expression of intense anxiety. 'What do you advise?' he asked.

'We certainly can't do much at night,' Segrue answered. 'Still — '

'See here,' Askew interposed. 'My opinion is that Mrs. Rodman hasn't gone far from the camp. Why, it stands to reason that in her condition she wouldn't have wandered over the mountains. As like as not she'll come to her right mind and make her way back as soon as it grows dark.

'You've spent the whole day looking for her without results, and it stands to reason nothing can be done at night. No use raising the country for a night hunt that'll simply tire out the searchers and stop them from putting in their best work during the day.

'What I'd advise is this. Build a big bonfire on the lawn, so that she'll see it if she's anywhere near. Then wait till the first thing tomorrow, and if she's not back then we'll organize a search party and scour every square foot of territory for five miles around.'

'I think that's about the only thing to

do,' Judge Segrue acknowledged.

Materials for the bonfire were at once collected and soon a huge pyramid of fire was leaping up from the lawn, with Alphonse in attendance. Afterward came a wretched meal, presided over by Mrs. Hollis, and eaten almost in silence. Hollis himself seemed equally broken down by the events of the preceding twenty hours.

'With your permission, Mr. Hollis,' said Askew, 'I'm going to sleep in that empty bungalow next door tonight.'

He jerked his head toward the one on the left, between the clubhouse and Carberry's.

'Yes — certainly — whichever one you prefer, Mr. Askew,' answered Hollis mechanically. 'There's — there's no news of Mr. Winscombe, I suppose?'

'Nothing so far. The roads are being watched. He'll have to show himself in a day or two.'

Hollis shook his head compassionately and said nothing. His wife went quickly to her room, her handkerchief to her eyes. Hollis was following her when Askew said:

'By the way, Mr. Hollis, I've told the men there's no need to watch the bungalow. I've done all the work there is to be done there, except putting those papers together, and I guess nobody's likely to steal 'em.'

Hollis nodded and left the room. Askew's eyes met Judge Segrue's in a steady, momentary, unflinching gaze.

I wonder just how much the old boy knows, the detective reflected.

Whatever Judge Segrue knew or suspected, he kept to himself. But there was no more chance of sleep for him that night than the night before. He lay on his bed, half dressed, in a deathly stillness. And, as he lay there, feeling the hours slip past him, he knew that he was expecting an even more startling denouement than the events of the night before. Somewhere the tangled skein that fate had woven about them was about to break.

At last the feeling became so strong and imminent that he rose from his bed, slipped on his coat and shoes, and waited. Each minute seemed on leash, straining toward the culmination. It was still two hours from dawn, but the moon had set, the night was pitch dark, and all about him was the same stillness of unearthly silence, in which he seemed to feel the play of conflicting human passions, locked like wrestlers, but breaking, breaking . . .

Suddenly the denouement came in the form of a single rifle shot from the direction of Rodman's bungalow, followed by a volley. Someone was shouting. Instantly the Judge was on his feet. He leaped down the stairs, past the closed door of the Hollis apartment, and ran into the darkness. The flickering of the dying bonfire hardly illuminated it any longer.

The light in Rodman's bungalow had been snapped on. Detective Askew was standing in the doorway, reeling, blood streaming from his head, but he held fast by the wrist a struggling woman who fought with him desperately — *Queenie!*

Upon the Judge's heels came Hollis and the two servants. They reached the bungalow together. There had been a mad struggle inside. The furniture was displaced, and the floor strewn with papers.

Hollis uttered a cry and leaped at the

detective, who released Queenie, and, as the manufacturer caught his wife in his arms, Askew quickly wiped the blood that streamed from a jagged scalp wound, then deliberately drew a pistol and held it to Hollis's head.

'I arrest *you* for the murder of Eustace Rodman,' he said grimly.

And, as Judge Segrue would have intervened: '*Step back!*' he shouted harshly. 'You *knew* it. I was wise to your game when you declined to help me.' Without letting the pistol in his hand waver an inch, he turned his glance upon the astonished Frenchmen.

'I call upon you men to guard this prisoner,' he said. 'If he escapes or kills himself, you'll be responsible.' His eyes flickered grimly on Queenie Hollis's face.

'I want *you* as an accessory,' he said. Queenie Hollis clung to her husband's arm.

'It's all right; I'll tell everything,' she answered in a restrained, mechanical voice.

As Hollis, who appeared completely stupefied by the turn of events, glanced at her, Judge Segrue took a step toward her.

'Yes, tell him everything, Mrs. Hollis,' he said quietly. 'And I'll add something. Let's go into the clubroom.'

6

Escaping from the bungalow, Chester Winscombe paddled with desperation across the width of the lake until he reached the shadows of the trees against the farther shore. His plunge from the scene of the murder had been designed to give him the appearance of guilt; the sole thought in his mind had been to take the proof of murder on himself and to save Mary.

Beyond that first, immediate instinctive act, his mind had not functioned; but now, as he paddled across the lake with furious energy, it began to work with tremendous speed. He realized that Mary would admit her guilt rather than allow him to be sent to the gallows, or to life imprisonment.

He must, then, make good his escape. So long as he was at liberty, Mary was safe, and would accept his sacrifice. Winscombe knew that the news would have been telephoned everywhere long before he could get free. His only chance was to strike boldly across the forest toward some distant point, avoiding roads and settlements.

He knew that a man can live comfortably for at least two weeks without food, performing quite normal activities the while, once the pangs and faintness of the first day or two have ceased. He decided to aim north, cross the Canadian border, and, covering fifteen to twenty miles a day, to emerge from the forest region miles away from the scene of the tragedy.

But, as he paused within the shadows of the trees, feeling the first fury of his nervous impulse spent, his arm fell to his side. Something wet dripped on his hand. He discovered that his sleeve was soaked with blood.

Then he perceived a little tear in the cloth. He took off his coat, found his shirt saturated, and discovered a neat groove through the fleshy part of his arm.

Rodman, in spinning round, had discharged his weapon blindly, and the chance shot had struck him, but in the excitement to which his mind was keyed he had not been aware of it.

He cut away the blood-soaked arm of his shirt, and bound up the wound with his handkerchief. Though it had bled a good deal, it was comparatively slight in character; it was obvious, however, that the arm was definitely out of commission.

With his sound arm Winscombe guided the canoe into the shallows, and beached it there. He would be unable to use it again, but then, he would have no further need of it.

He tore away the tail of his shirt and improvised a sling for his arm, which was now beginning to throb painfully, and then set off. A trail ran here to the water's edge, uniting with the main road some distance away, and branching off up the mountain. Winscombe had spent two weeks at the camp the year before, and was roughly acquainted with the locality. Beyond the ridge of mountains lay a wilderness, traversed by paths leading northward toward the boundary.

He picked up the trail and doggedly began the ascent of the mountain. But he had not gone very far before he felt his strength failing him. He had lost a good deal of blood. Half a mile or so from the edge of the lake he was forced to stop. The mountains still towered above him, and the trail was growing steeper every moment. After endeavoring in vain to continue his journey, he crept into a thicket beside the trail, flung himself down, and lapsed into unconsciousness.

There ensued a night of delirium. What happened, Winscombe never knew. He was only dimly aware of trying to continue his journey, of the agonizing fear of discovery, with Mary's consequent inculpation; he came to himself to find the risen sun staring at him through the trees, and the forest all about him. His arm was badly swollen, and the wound throbbed like knife stabs. Thirst tortured him.

Under the mad impulse to find water he plunged down the mountain slope, expecting to discover the trail, but each step led him further and further astray. When at last he stopped through exhaustion he realized that he was hopelessly lost. His watch was gone, and he could only vaguely guess his position from the sun.

That day was a period of delirium, during which he staggered on mechanically, sinking to the ground and rising again and again in the hope of finding water. It was not until after sunset that his mental activities revived. At dark he found the pole star, recast his direction, and set out in the direction of the lake once more. And at last, when he felt that he could go no farther, he found it suddenly.

He flung himself upon his face at the edge and drank furiously. He lay back, exhausted, but momentarily appeased. His mind was clear now, and he realized that in his condition his plans had become impossible. He must die there, and, dying, he would bear the guilt of Rodman's murder forever.

Then he saw Mary!

She was coming toward him up the trail, her dress torn and covered with burrs, her hair hanging about her face, and he looked at her stupidly, almost believing that she was a phantom of his brain. But it was a phantom of flesh and blood that ran to him and clung to him, and then, kneeling beside him, removed the blood-stained bandage from his arm and substituted a new one, torn from her underskirt.

'Chester, I have been searching for you since morning,' she sobbed beside him. 'I knew that you were wounded, and I was in agony. Why did you kill him? Oh, the pity of it! What folly, what madness, Chester!' She began laughing hysterically.

'Mary, didn't you — didn't *you* shoot him?' cried Winscombe in stupefaction.

She snatched her hands away from his.

'Oh, how can you say that to me?' she asked. 'Are you trying to incriminate me, when I would have given my life to save you? *You* shot him, Chester, and you shot him down in his tracks like a dog, without a chance, from *outside* the bungalow!'

Winscombe felt his blood turning to ice under her vituperation. In his weakness he reflected bitterly that he had become a hunted fugitive for her, while she was trying to place the guilt on him.

'I never fired a single shot! You *know*

that I have, and never would, lie to you!'

Suddenly Mary put out her hands and caught him by the shoulders. An access of furious energy made her slim body almost as strong as a man's.

'Do you swear that, Chester?' she cried. 'Is that true? Do you swear you didn't murder him?'

'What's the use of swearing?' asked Winscombe hopelessly. 'Mary, the instant before he died I heard you struggling with him. I saw your shadow on the blind.'

She stared at him piteously. '*My shadow!*' she whispered. 'Oh, God, Chester, it — it was not mine!'

He seized her by the arm in wild excitement. 'Not yours, Mary?' he cried. 'Then — then it must have been — '

But she had sunk down beside him, covering her face in a wild outburst of grief, and for a long time he was unable to calm her. Yet, when at length her sobbing ceased, and she drew her hands away, she had grown composed again.

She drew his head upon her knee, and they crouched there together. Winscombe slept from weariness, but all night Mary watched him with sleepless eyes. When at length he awoke to the touch of the girl's hand on his shoulder there was the sense of dawn in the air, though it was still dark.

'Chester, do you think you can walk?' asked Mary, bending over him.

He struggled to his feet, and they set off slowly along the trail. Winscombe took the lead, overcoming his weakness with a strong effort of will. Their progress was infinitely slow over the rugged trail, encumbered with roots and stones.

At last, looking beyond the trees, they could see the camp faintly outlined against the darkness, behind the flicker of the dying fire.

And suddenly a volley of shots rang out.

Instantly Mary seized Winscombe by his good arm, and almost dragged him back into the underbrush. They crouched there, breathing heavily, and seeking each other's faces in the darkness.

Minutes of suspense went by. All hope had vanished. Whatever it was that had happened, they at least must wait until another night had closed on them. At last Winscombe rose.

'We'll have to go back,' he said wearily.

And, as he spoke, a figure loomed and slammed headlong upon him out of the darkness.

The two closed in a mad tussle, though neither could see the other's face. For fifteen seconds Winscombe fought his invisible antagonist, while the girl, unable to intervene, could only watch the struggle in helpless frenzy. Then, summoning his last strength, Winscombe flung his assailant to the ground. He lay there, making no attempt to rise. Mary ran to Winscombe, who caught and held her.

'Chester, come!' she sobbed, tugging at him. 'Quick, before he recovers.'

Suddenly she screamed:

'*Chester*, he's stabbed you. There's — *there's blood all over you!*'

Winscombe looked into her face vacantly, and suddenly collapsed into unconsciousness beside his antagonist.

7

Inside the clubhouse Judge Segrue, in contradiction of his former decision to take no part in the proceedings, had assumed the dominant role, while Detective Askew, reduced to playing a subsidiary one, faced him and the Hollises.

'I'm willing to explain, Judge, and to listen,' he said, 'because I've got these people sure, and the best thing will be to drop all pretenses and come straight through with the facts. I guess you've known all along, and are now ready to aid the cause of justice. And if it's shown to be something less than murder, nobody will be more pleased than me.'

He turned toward the Hollises.

'You worked it well enough,' he said, 'but you gave yourselves dead away. In the first place, about snapping off the light in Rodman's bungalow — well, that man Pierre, naturally he thought it was Mrs. Rodman he saw, but it wasn't. It was *you*,

Mrs. Hollis. There were traces of prints all over the switch button, and, planted clear on top of them, and ten times as firm, there were finger and thumb prints that weren't Mrs. Rodman's at all.'

Hollis, who had been watching the detective's face intently, turned and glanced at Queenie, then half rose, uttering an inarticulate syllable. Judge Segrue stepped quickly from his chair to his side, and placed his hand on his shoulder, whispering something.

He resumed his seat, and Askew continued:

'Well, next we've found young Winscombe's pistol, and no shot had been fired out of it. Whoever murdered Rodman — not that it's in doubt — used that rifle in the hall and cleaned it afterward. Easy enough to slip in in the dark and souse it with oil.

'It stands to reason young Winscombe couldn't have put back the rifle and cleaned it if he ran straight down to the lake and paddled away. No, his part's clear enough. He thought that Mrs. Rodman had murdered her husband, and he made his getaway to shield her.'

Suddenly the manufacturer sprang from his chair with a growl of fury. Instantly the detective had him covered with his pistol, and, after a moment of hesitation, he sat down again.

'You may as well hear it out,' continued Askew. 'You two were working hand in glove, but for different reasons. I'll come to that in a minute. When I learned that Mr. Hollis tried to get into the bungalow after the murder, and that you wouldn't stand for it, Judge, I guessed if I withdrew the guard he'd be back again tonight. That's what I was waiting for, but you were a little too quick for me, and so I've got *this* to thank you for.'

He touched the bandage round his head.

Hollis stood up slowly.

'Do you mean to say it was *I* attacked you tonight?' he demanded.

'Well, I guess so.'

'Did you recognize me?'

'I caught your wife in the bungalow. I guess that's sufficient,' retorted Askew. 'And I was saying you two had different reasons. I'll take that up now. One of you shot Rodman, and I guess you're man enough, Mr. Hollis, not to squeal if I put it on you instead of this lady. You shot him because you'd had business troubles with him, and wanted him out of the way. He had you by the throat, according to those carbon copies of the letters he'd written you. That's why you wanted those papers sealed — and that's why you tried to get back into the bungalow to take 'em a few minutes after the murder — and again tonight. And Mrs. Hollis was hand in glove with you, but for a different reason, and one which I guess you don't know.

'It'll have to come out,' he went on reluctantly, 'and I guess you may as well know now. Rodman was your wife's *lover* — '

With a single bound Hollis was out of his chair and at the detective's throat.

But before Askew could fire — if he had *meant* to fire — Judge Segrue, who had been watching Hollis like a lynx, had sprung between them. With surprising strength he forced the two apart.

'*Sit down!*' he cried, grappling with the manufacturer, who in inarticulate rage, was trying to hurl himself upon Askew again. 'That was a lie — and we're going to prove it was a lie — but, he didn't know.'

And by sheer strength he forced the manufacturer into a chair, where he lay exhausted, glaring at the detective.

With a sudden chivalrous impulse Askew stepped forward, shook the cartridges out of his automatic, and laid it on the table. He turned to the Judge.

'There *was* a package of letters — love letters from a woman — in Rodman's case,' he said. 'They were signed by a fictitious name, but the writing was Mrs. Hollis's — *letter* for *letter*. I compared the writing with that on the envelopes of the letters she'd written for the post.

'Rodman was holding them over her, in case Mr. Hollis showed fight. That's why she went to Rodman's bungalow, meaning to steal them after Mr. Hollis had murdered him. And that, maybe, is why Mrs. Rodman was an accessory — you can't tell what women will do — '

'One moment,' the Judge interposed. 'What name was signed to those letters, Mr. Askew?'

'Nora Brayton.'

Hollis's cry rapped through the room like a pistol shot. Queenie turned toward him.

'Yes, I am Nora Brayton,' she said quietly. 'I am the woman of whom I've heard you speak in connection with Eustace Rodman, and always with contempt and bitterness. I heard you speak of her so on the evening of his death. When I heard you say that, I resolved to kill him, rather than lose your love.

'I am one of Eustace Rodman's victims. I am the woman who shot him years ago, who went to the penitentiary for him. I came out, and found myself divorced, alone, friendless. I built up my life again, met you, loved you, Lonnie, married you, hoping my secret would forever remain secure, but risking all because I loved you, and because I trusted in your love for me.

'The inevitable day came when Rodman and I came face to face. He recognized me. He told me that the secret of my past was safe — so long as he chose. He told his wife — that was one of the diabolical ways he had of hurting her. Mary is true as steel. She sought me out, made me her friend and confidant; she never believed in my guilt.

'You recognized me, Judge Segrue, and, though you have never told me so, unwittingly you let me know. But I always knew you were my friend and would never betray me. I was never afraid of you, and I think you always believed in my innocence.'

'I know it, and I declare it to you now, Mrs. Hollis,' said the Judge with emotion.

'The time came,' continued Queenie, 'when my husband and Eustace Rodman became business enemies. Then he began to threaten me with betrayal, unless I used my influence with my husband in his behalf. As time went on, his threats grew more serious. At last the time arrived when denunciation was imminent. He told me that he was coming into camp to have it out with my husband; that, in the last resource, he would save himself by showing him those letters.

'They were lies — forgeries — lies! I swear it *again*, as I swore all those years ago! Forgeries, done so skilfully that they once deceived a court of law, and could never now be disproved. I went to his bungalow at night, mad, desperate, resolved to kill him. I took a revolver with me. Mary did not expect me, but she did not intervene. She saw that I was past reason, and that no act of any human being's except his own could save Eustace Rodman this time.

'I begged and pleaded with him. He laughed at me, always returning the same answer: my safety depended on my ability to persuade my husband not to use his advantage. Then — then — '

Suddenly she broke down in tearless sobs that choked her utterance. She stretched out her arms blindly toward her husband; but Hollis, huddled up in his chair like an old man, only looked at her fixedly, and made no movement toward her.

Judge Segrue crossed to her and placed his hand on her shoulder.

'So that is why you killed Eustace

Rodman,' he said gently. 'No jury will convict — no jury on earth.'

She looked at him more calmly.

'I didn't,' she said quietly. 'I didn't. I wish I had. He had had experience of me; he knew I had a revolver; suddenly he snatched it out of the hand I held behind my back. We struggled, and — someone fired. He fired wildly and fell. Then I saw Chester Winscombe standing in the doorway, his pistol pointed at him — '

The Judge looked at her in pitying surprise, but did not contradict her. And suddenly she tottered forward and flung herself upon her knees at Hollis's feet.

Judge Segrue bent his gaze on him, as if trying by force of will to draw the words of pardon from his mouth, but Hollis only sat silent, huddled up in his chair.

Askew cleared his throat.

'I knew about that case — the Brayton case,' he said. 'Of course, if Mrs. Hollis states that she alone was responsible for Rodman's death, why — '

'I wasn't,' said Queenie simply.

'There's no one else,' said Askew quietly, 'except your husband, and — '

There was the stamping of feet outside the clubroom. Mary Rodman stood on the threshold, supporting Winscombe, who, ghastly pale, leaned against the jamb. Behind them came Pierre and Alphonse, supporting the body of a man.

It was Carberry.

They laid him on the sofa. Blood was oozing slowly, from two gaping bullet wounds in his breast, and it was clear at once that he was dying. He opened his eyes and looked about him, recognized Queenie wistfully, and seemed to call her.

At the sight of him Judge Segrue suddenly staggered and clutched the head of the couch to save himself from falling.

'My God!' he muttered. 'It can't be! But, it is! God, it's Brayton! And I didn't know him till now!'

Brayton's lips moved. He was speaking, so softly that they kneeled beside him to catch his words.

'I killed Rodman,' he whispered. 'I never knew he was here — never suspected till — what you said — '

He was looking at the Judge.

'You said he deserved to die. And that

those — letters were forgeries. I — went to kill him. And I — wanted those letters to make sure. I was mad at the sight of her. We knew each other. I — had to kill him and to get them. I — killed him, but he — I mean Winscombe — frightened me away. I — went back last night and — got this. That's all. I — I believe in her — '

His head fell back. The eyes closed.

Judge Segrue placed his arm beneath the head, which moved slowly once or twice. A long sigh came from the lips. Judge Segrue spread his handkerchief over the face. He rose to his feet; his hand fell on Hollis's shoulder.

'He believed in her,' he said gravely. 'You must believe, too.'

The silence of death within the clubroom was broken by the sound of wheels outside. A wagon stopped before the door. Out of it stepped a middle aged man, who came quickly up the steps, and halted in the entrance in stupefaction at the scene.

Judge Segrue went quickly to him and shook him by the hand.

'I'm glad you came, Pettibone,' he said. He turned to Hollis.

'This is my friend who received the confession from the forger,' he said. 'Mr. Pettibone, will you come with me and Mr. Hollis and tell him what you know about that, and — make him believe?'

And Mary, a half hour later, kneeled at the unconscious Chester's bedside, and drew his arm about her. 'He believes,' she whispered into his ear. 'Shall we two believe — forever?'

We do hope that you have enjoyed reading this large print book.

Did you know that all of our titles are available for purchase?

We publish a wide range of high quality large print books including:
Romances, Mysteries, Classics
General Fiction
Non Fiction and Westerns

Special interest titles available in large print are:
The Little Oxford Dictionary
Music Book, Song Book
Hymn Book, Service Book

Also available from us courtesy of Oxford University Press:
Young Readers' Dictionary
(large print edition)
Young Readers' Thesaurus
(large print edition)

For further information or a free brochure, please contact us at:
Ulverscroft Large Print Books Ltd.,
The Green, Bradgate Road, Anstey,
Leicester, LE7 7FU, England.
Tel: (00 44) **0116 236 4325**
Fax: (00 44) **0116 234 0205**

Other titles in the
Linford Mystery Library:

A QUESTION OF GUILT

Tony Gleeson

Dane Spilwell, a brilliant surgeon, stands accused of the brutal murder of his wife. The evidence against him is damning, his guilt almost a foregone conclusion. Two red-haired women will determine his ultimate fate. One, a mysterious lady in emeralds, may be the key to clearing him of the crime — if only she can be located. The other, Detective Jilly Garvey, began by doggedly working to convict him — but now finds herself doubting his culpability . . .

TWEAK THE DEVIL'S NOSE

Richard Deming

Driving to the El Patio club to see his girlfriend Fausta Moreni, the establishment's proprietor, private investigator Manville Moon does not expect to be witness to a murder. As he steps from his car outside the club, he hears a gun suddenly roar from the bushes close behind him. Walter Lancaster, the lieutenant governor of the neighbouring state of Illinois, has been shot! The assassination will not only make headlines all over the country, but also place the lives of Moon and Fausta in deadly danger . . .

THE MAN WITH THE CAMERA EYES

Victor Rousseau

Investigative lawyer Langton has solved many bizarre cases with the help of his friend Peter Crewe, who possesses such an extraordinary photographic memory that he never forgets a face. Here Langton relates twelve stories featuring audacious jewel robberies, scientific geniuses gone mad and bad, and cold-blooded murder served up via amusement park rides, craftily concealed explosives, and hot air balloons. In each, the Man with the Camera Eyes provides the observations and deductions that are crucial to the solution of the mystery — often risking his own life in the process . . .

THE SEPIA SIREN KILLER

Richard A. Lupoff

Prior to World War II, black actors were restricted to minor roles in mainstream films — though there was a 'black' Hollywood that created films with all-black casts for exhibition to black audiences. When a cache of long-lost films is discovered by cinema researchers, the aged director Edward 'Speedy' MacReedy appears to reclaim his place in film history. But insurance investigator Hobart Lindsey and homicide officer Marvia Plum soon find themselves enmeshed in a frightening web of arson and murder with its roots deep in the tragic events of a past era . . .

KILLING COUSINS

Fletcher Flora

Suburban housewife Willie Hogan is selfish, bored, and beautiful, passing her time at the country club and having casual affairs. Her husband Howard doesn't seem to care particularly — until one night she comes home from a party to discover he has packed his things and intends to leave her for good. Panicked, Willie grabs Howard's gun and shoots him dead. With the help of her current paramour, Howard's clever cousin Quincy, the body is disposed of — but unbeknownst to either of them, their problems are only just beginning . . .

A CORNISH VENGEANCE

Rena George

Silas Venning, millionaire owner of a luxury yacht company, is found hanged in a remote Cornish wood. It looks like suicide — but his widow, celebrated artist Laura Anstey, doesn't think so. She enlists Loveday Ross to help prove her suspicions. But there can be no doubts about the killing of Venning's former employee Brian Penrose — not when he's mown down by a hit-and-run driver right in front of Loveday's boyfriend, DI Sam Kitto. Could they be dealing with *two* murders?